C000062549

GRAPE CITY

ALSO BY KEVIN L. DONIHE

Shall We Gather at the Garden?
Ocean of Lard (w/ Carlton Mellick III)
The Greatest Fucking Moment In Sports
House of Houses

GRAPE CITY

Kevin L. Donihe

ERASERHEAD PRESS
Portland, OR

ERASERHEAD PRESS
205 NE BRYANT
PORTLAND, OR 97211

WWW.ERASERHEADPRESS.COM

ISBN: 1-9339295-1-0

Copyright © 2006 by Kevin L Donihe
Cover art copyright © 2006 by Lucas Aguirre

All rights reserved. No part of this book may be reproduced or transmitted in any form or by any means, electronic or mechanical, including photocopying, recording, or by any information storage and retrieval system, without the written consent of the publisher, except where permitted by law.

Printed in the USA.

This book is dedicated to:

Christopher Clay
Jarrod Sword
(and, of course, my family)

Author's Note:

Well here it is, the first book finished since co-writing *Ocean of Lard* back in the summer of 2003. I have been bad. Very, very bad. And I apologize for it; really don't know what came over me, other than I couldn't write anything worth squat for a while. No matter what I thought I typed, it appeared on the computer screen as, *"Karharga fluffen-ummama klabbo flabzoomen."* (This includes personal email, which explains why people stopped writing and no longer invited me to house parties and ice cream socials...

... I *really* missed the ice cream socials, but I'm going to one right after I finish this note, so things are starting to look up.)

At any rate, I won't go so long between books again. I was lost in some sort of weird, spongy cavern, but I'm back now, and I've already written *House of Houses* and *The Greatest Fucking Moment in Sports*. The *Shall We Gather at the Garden?* redux is in the bag, too—and I hope to have four more books ready by or before May 2007.

Time will tell if I make it (but, unless some vital part of me shrivels up and dies, I'll at least come very, very close).

—Kevin L. Donihe
April 03, 2006

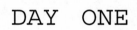

DAY ONE

CHARLES HATED THE lights, especially those around the fry-warmer. They heated the metallic pins in his face and irritated his skin. The sensation—coupled with the pings, clicks, pops, and fizzes of the machinery—made him want to tear his face off. He could live without a face. It was vanity alone that kept his nails from clawing at pale, spongy flesh and his fists from throwing the resulting debris into the deep fryer.

He longed for the trappings of old. His clothes were nothing like the magenta, neo-metal Goth gear he'd previously worn. Charles missed the fire-forged chains. He yearned to once again feel the embrace of leather torn from the bodies of three-headed cows. His *Burger Hut* uniform just wasn't the same.

Charles tugged at the uniform. He felt like a dancing clown, a circus freak to stare at and mock. It wasn't right that a high-ranking minion in the Court of Hell should wear a white, pinstriped shirt with a happy, anthropomorphic burger patch stitched on the left breast. It wasn't right that he was forced to relinquish his old name. So beautiful it was; it rolled off the tongue and struck fear in all who heard it. 'Charles', however, struck fear in no one. He'd hoped, at the very least, that he might pick his own name—something Germanic with a lot of harsh consonant sounds—but that was never an option. 'Charles' was read from a list at the Grape City division of the *Bureau of Demonic Immigration*, and 'Charles' he became. Only Satan got to keep his original name after Hell closed.

The bubbling of oil was grating, but if Charles separated the sound from its source and spaced out, it became hypnotic. He stood above the fryer, dreaming of red, sandy shores and spiral shaped buildings that pierced a blue-black sky. A loud, repetitive beeping soon interrupted his reverie. He slid from his trance and smelled something burning. Charles looked down at the submerged basket and saw black, smoking fries.

In a panic, he tried to dump the basket. A hand fell upon his shoulder, and Charles spun around.

Manager Jim stared at him angrily.

"Damn it, Charles! This is the second time you've burned the fries this week!"

Charles' voice was deep, dirt-clotted: "Sorry, it won't happen again."

"That's what you said last time!" The manager shook a meaty finger back and forth. "But these fries sure as hell didn't burn themselves!"

"I accept full responsibility for my actions, sir." Charles cringed. It didn't feel right for a ninth circle demon to address any man as *sir*.

"One more time, Charles! *One more time!*"

"I understand. I'll make another batch."

"Not on your life; I'm moving you out front."

"But I hate dealing with people!" His eyes were fiery yet pleading. "You know this!"

"Yeah, and I also know how much those ruined fries cost. Now get to the counter!"

"But—"

Manager Jim's cheeks flushed. "*Get to the counter before I have to mess you up!*"

12

Though male, Charles curtsied and uttered the customary, "whatever pleasures you, sir." Employees who didn't were to be terminated on the spot.

Charles couldn't take that risk, so he swallowed what remained of his pride and slunk to the register. He already held two jobs, but those two put together weren't half as bad as working at *The Doughnut Kiosk* in the mall. His old boss was equally insufferable, but *The Burger Hut* offered more than just soggy doughnuts to eat. At the kiosk, he was forced to consume them, sometimes against his will.

The day had proven quiet. Only three sets of tables were filled, and no one had entered the restaurant in fifteen minutes; Monday afternoons were usually slow. Charles remained by the register—fist propped beneath his chin, staring at the ketchup dispenser—until a customer walked through the door.

The man faced him, a twenty-something frat guy complete with an Anders Beer T-Shirt, black sunglasses, deep-pocketed shorts, and sandals. He had a large cold sore above his lip, but that was customary. Sexually transmitted diseases had gone airborne.

Charles imagined himself ripping the frat guy's head off and shoving something horrible down his spurting neck stump. Instead, he gave his customary spiel: "Hello, my name is Charles. May I take your order, please?" He had considered adding 'fucking' between 'your' and 'order,' but decided against it.

The frat guy hummed and hawed and stared blankly at the menu for what, to Charles, seemed like an hour. Finally, he said, "I'll have two fries and two hamburgers with extra mayo and pickles."

"That'll be $8.56. *Pay now.*"

The guy handed him the money, and Charles breathed out a sigh. One customer was down, but others would surely follow. He noticed that a lot of people came into *The Burger Hut*—usually the same ones, day after day after day.

Once the frat guy found his seat, Charles returned to staring, this time at a napkin dispenser. Not a minute passed, however, before the guy left his seat and again stepped up to the counter.

"Hey, metalhead!" He slammed the fries down and leered. "Did you know these are cold?"

Charles' voice was a sonorous boom: "No."

"Well," the guy huffed. "*They are.*"

He touched the fries. "You are sadly mistaken."

"No, I'm not. Now give my money back and make me new fries!"

"I will *never* do these things."

"Hey, that's no—"

"*Never.*"

"But your policy—"

"*Fuck my policy.*"

"Wha—"

Charles waved his hand. The guy's shirt exploded, sending fragments hurtling in multiple directions. His belt buckle unfastened; shorts fell to the floor with a *whoosh*. The guy seemed at first surprised, and then embarrassed, as he stood in line wearing red tighty whities.

"That will teach you to mess with things from Hell!"

The frat guy clutched his manhood. "You can suck my dick, metalhead!" Then he paused, as though trying to find the right words. "*Faggot!*"

Charles clenched his fists. Black, sticky blood dripped

from them onto the counter, but the frat guy didn't notice this as he bent to pull up his shorts.

"No, it is you who will be sucking dick today."

Before the frat guy's shorts reached his knees, his penis stirred. Quickly, it overshot his underwear and became a raging boner. He turned to Charles: "You're doing this, aren't you!"

Charles said nothing, not even as the penis continued to grow, shooting past natural boundaries, further and further until it reached the guy's nose.

"Sweet Lord! It's not supposed to get that big!"

The member turned its lone eye towards him and hissed. The frat guy attempted to grab it, but it made a feint to the left and coiled, serpent-like, around his throat. He collapsed to the floor, eyes bulging as blood vessels exploded. His tongue, now blue, hung limply over his cheek.

Charles delighted in the sound of crunching cartilage. "Hope you don't mind swallowing," he said.

As the frat guy's choking spasms died away, the penis released its grip on his throat and shot into his mouth. It shattered front teeth before exiting the back of his head. Skull and brain matter sprayed out onto gray tiles.

* * * *

"My fries are gettin' colder, man. I don't got all day. Gimme new ones or things'll get personal."

Charles' fantasy world disintegrated. He had no idea how long he'd stood there, gazing into nothing.

In the past, he could have used the frat guy's penis as a weapon. It would have been a prosaic thing to do, but it would have also been just another rage-driven act. In Hell, darkness provided a counterpoint to the light and made it visible. That, he thought, was a noble calling, one notably absent on Earth.

He wondered if the human sphere was corrupting him, turning him into another stupid or frothing animal. It had already canceled most of his powers, so he would have to deal with the frat guy on frat guy terms. His face folded into a grimace. "Whatever pleases you—"

Before he could finish, a blur streaked across the counter. It was Manager Jim.

"Gotta problem with the fries, bitch?"

"Hey, I ain't no—"

Manager Jim punched him hard in the gut. The frat guy bent forward and clutched his stomach. Manager Jim took advantage of this and wrapped him in a headlock, pummeling his face as he squeezed.

"Our fries aren't good enough. That *is* what you're saying, right?"

Charles turned to the customers. He expected they'd either join in or ignore the melee. All continued to stuff fries and burgers and nuggets into faces that were not always their own.

Manager Jim brought forth a switchblade. He clicked it open. "Come back again and I'll ram this through one side of your neck and out the other. Do you understand?"

The frat guy shook his head.

"Say it!" Manager Jim pressed the knife deeper, drawing blood. "Say you understand!"

"I—I understand."

Manager Jim licked the blood trail from the frat guy's neck, then ran his tongue up and down his face, smearing it red. "You don't want to know what I could do to you, so leave before I do it." He grabbed a handful of the guy's ass. "All night long."

Manager Jim released him. The frat guy sprinted across the restaurant and out the door, almost tripping over two copulating bodies that writhed on the sidewalk. Manager Jim watched until he was out of sight. Then he straightened his shirt and tie and hopped over the counter. He turned to Charles.

"I saw the way you were looking. I know you wanted to lay into him, to taste his fear." He licked away the blood still on his lips. "I'm glad you held back, though. I'd hate to have to fire your ass."

"I would never abuse a customer." Charles was too afraid to add 'though I wanted to strangle him with his cock.'

"Good. You'll have that right if and when you make manager, but you'll have to take me out first, turtledove. And I won't go quietly into the good night."

He just nodded.

"Now get back to the register. Oh, and I've penciled you in for register duty next Saturday and Sunday, too." Manager Jim grinned, showing off teeth he'd filed into neat points. "I'm sure you won't mind."

* * * *

The rest of the day was relatively quiet. A few people were molested in the bathroom and a woman had committed suicide by stuffing an entire Happy Burger into her throat before packing it down with her fist; Charles had never seen a jaw open so wide. He was glad he hadn't been responsible for her cleanup. She just went into the dumpster out back with the rest—and her body wasn't at all hacked-up or bloody—but it still made him sick each time such a task was assigned to him.

* * * *

When his shift was over, Charles punched out. He didn't see Jim before he left. He had shut himself up in his office again. Charles heard odd sloshing sounds from behind the door marked 'Manager' and assumed he was busy doing whatever he did after closing hours. Charles had never been inside the office—it wasn't allowed—but he'd once seen the door cracked a bit and, beyond, strewn pieces of meat that didn't resemble anything the restaurant served.

Once outside, he sidestepped the still-copulating couple. An advertisement plastered to a building caught his eye. Charles hated the thing and vowed he'd never look again, but his eyes felt drawn to it whenever he left *The Burger Hut*. He wondered if it featured subliminal encoding, perhaps some sort of electronic control device. That possibility seemed less and less absurd as time passed.

He turned and saw more and more plastered ads. No building was spared; even windows and doors had been covered to make room for them. Once, as he passed a ground-level advert, he'd heard people screaming and howling behind the ad that blocked their exit.

The ads were a confusing nuisance. Not one seemed to correspond with the showcased product. They usually featured some or another hellish scene with taglines like 'Get That Horror-Rape Feeling' or 'Hack-Slam, Fuck Yeah.' Children's products were invariably advertised with 'Terror-Hack the Bang-Slammers.'

The particularly hated billboard featured an autopsy scene. The forensic pathologist was eating a bowl of *Flang-Os*—a frosted bear-shaped cereal—as he stood behind a woman on a slab. Her scalp had been peeled back and the top of her skull sawn off. It appeared as though the doctor was inserting himself into her brain, but his position left some ambiguity.

Charles tore his eyes from the billboard, but again found himself staring, this time at two oldsters sitting on a bench across the street. People watching had disturbing and sometimes dire consequences, but he did it just the same, like a hungry rubbernecker at an auto accident.

The man and woman were both engrossed in the paper. A hanged body swung in the trees above them. As they sat, peacefully enough, a teenaged guy approached, all twitchy and jittery. Lumpy fluid dripped from his ears, a sure sign of Mexotrexic-8 intoxication.

Charles listened to their conversation as he passed.

The young man: "Bitch, give me the paper. I must read it."

The old woman: "Not until you ask nicely."

"Please, bitch, kindly hand me the paper."

"Not good enough." She waved him away. "Go and get your own."

"But I want yours."

The woman turned to the man beside her. "Go horror-slam that guy and take his paper. Leave mine alone."

The old man: "Whatever."

The young guy walked to the old man, bending down to survey his paper. He poked it with his thumb a few times and then said, "Nope, his paper's not good enough."

The woman harrumphed and pulled a gun from the folds of her oversized sweater. She leaned forward, pressing the barrel into the teen's chest. "Fucking kids these days. Never satisfied with anything." Then she fired. When she made like she was going to violate the corpse, Charles turned away.

He'd heard that there had been other types—better types—of people before Hell closed. Those types had all gone away. He didn't know if he would have liked them—he'd never met them—so, however difficult, he gave them the benefit of the doubt.

Charles walked the rest of the way home, head down. He didn't see people that way, just the occasional passing shoe or leg, but often noted other things—red smears on the sidewalk, chunky wet things that looked suspiciously like organs, even a few severed limbs that had yet to be disposed of by waste management crews.

* * * *

Charles entered the stairwell that led to his apartment above *The Machine Shop*, which he'd first thought was some sort of repair place. It wasn't until his microwave broke after living there a month that he realized it was a brothel for people into electronics.

The staircase was dirty and grimy, but was also quiet. There was a second unit to the left of his, but it had been empty since he moved in.

At the top of the stairs, he unlocked the door and pushed it open. His apartment smelled stale, and it reminded him of everything he missed in hell. So vibrant and alive, it was nothing like this place where time seemed to stand still and rot on its feet. Peeling white walls and old gray carpeting. Sagging ceilings and leaky pipes. Never had his accommodations been more depressing.

Charles fell onto the sofa. He reached over the make-shift coffee table—an egg crate—for his laptop. He'd bought it at a pawnshop two weeks earlier from a greasy, white-beater sporting man with dirty nails. The floppy disk drive didn't work and three of the keys stuck, but it sufficed.

He booted it up, waited, and logged onto the Internet. It had seemed like a promising thing when he first heard about it, but that was before he realized that it consisted of porn, pictures of dead people, business sites (which usually also featured porn and pictures of dead people), message boards, and email. Nothing else. Email wasn't bad, though. He could always ignore the grisly pop-ups, and he knew which boards to steer clear from by their titles.

Charles logged onto the board for displaced demons. No new activity. He almost welcomed the silence. Attitudes there were usually gloomy—lots of bitching and moaning, nary a positive voice in the bunch. Still, it was nice to hear from his kind. He hardly ever saw them since, according to *The Demonic Assimilation Acts*, only a single demon could reside in a particular city at any given time.

Charles checked his email and found nothing but junk, mostly Spam advertising new drugs or overpriced killing machines. One even invited him to enlarge his penis, but he figured twenty-six inches was good enough. In Hell, he'd been 'average'. On Earth, however, he was gargantuan, freakish. Charles was stunned when, early on, a group of men removed their raincoats and waved their peckers at him. So miniscule and impotent, just thinking about them made him ill.

He wound up deleting the penis advert, plus four hundred and sixty-five other messages. Then he decided to write Satan, which would save his Internet experience from being a total bust. It had been a while since he'd heard from his old boss, and, truth be told, he was getting worried.

Dear Satan:

You've been quiet these past few weeks. How are you doing? Find a job yet? And how's Cerebus? Is your landlord still complaining about him?

Me? Well, I've had better days...

Sorry if that sounded vague or depressing, but it's true. I can't find anything here for me, but that doesn't mean I should quit looking, right?

On a lighter note, I picked up an old B-52s CD at the pawnshop a few days ago. It was wedged between a shelf and a wall, so I just took it. Have you heard the B-52s? If not, I could burn you a copy and drop it in the mail. I imagine it's a hard-to-find item, and my finding it was just a lucky fluke. There's not a drop of art or culture in this stupid town.

Anyway, I think you'd like it. Might even take your mind off all the bad things. :)

Well, that's all for now. Write back when you can.

— Charles

He hit 'send', thought about checking the displaced demon board again, but turned the computer off instead. Then he looked up at the ceiling and wondered what he might do with the remainder of his night.

Ultimately, he turned to the TV. It sometimes made the world seem far away. Charles had even started to enjoy sitcoms, chuckling at ditzy housewives and their precocious children. He just didn't like it when the humor stopped and the hacking began. His favorite show was *The Swiss Family Swayze*—partly because its actors had yet to be raped or murdered on-screen—but that wouldn't be on again until next week.

Once the sitcom he finally settled on ended, Charles turned to the news channel. It was a bit dull. In the past, a part would fall off or gas would escape from one or both of the swinging anchor-corpses. That always made for good ratings, as people would watch in hopes that something would fall or that they'd hear a sound resembling a fart. Charles hadn't seen or heard anything like that in a while—the corpses were well past the swollen stage. In fact, it was hard to tell which anchor was Tim and which was Jane. Their clothing had long ago fallen off, and decay had rendered both sexless.

He'd heard that they'd hung themselves. Others said that someone had done the hanging for them. Charles wasn't sure what to believe. They were dead when he entered the human realm, although they'd been much fresher then. There'd also been a makeshift sign on the wall, visible between the bodies—a piece of typing paper scrawled with red, drippy letters. He hadn't seen it in years and figured the tape that held it must have gotten old and fallen off.

LET THIS BE A LESSON TO YOU

it had said.

The news began to bore him. He flicked through the stations, past a repeat showing of *The Swiss Family Swayze* and a few other interchangable shows until he reached the religious network. It was interesting to watch, in a weird, hard-to-express way. Charles looked on, slightly bemused, as the slick, white-suited preacher screamed through the TV. Foam flew from his lips as his hands flailed.

"Who can say one hasn't taken the hose of another man?" He shouted. "We are all sinners, sinners in the same boat sinking fifty feet from a badger infested shore!"

The audience fell silent. Their eyes rolled back in their heads and foam much like the stuff flying from the preacher's mouth erupted from various orifices. That froth soon turned red.

The preacher droned on. "I tell you that you must hear this name and see this image to enter Paradise. Look at it. Gaze at it. Spin around and around with it. Suck in the white light. Do it. Suck in the white light. Enter Paradise today."

Charles caught himself sucking in the white light—it was so easy—but he made himself snap out of it.

If he'd sucked in the white light, it would have been the end of him.

He shut off the TV.

* * * *

Charles spent the next few hours sitting on an old, threadbare sofa. Each time he managed to close his eyes and Zen-out, he'd hear banging or throbbing from *The Machine Shop* downstairs.

He soon figured that he'd rest better in bed than on the

sofa. It was only 10:00 P.M. and tomorrow was his day off, but the night held no promise.

In the bedroom, he stripped off his *Burger Hut* uniform and fell into bed without removing the covers. He stared up at the surveillance camera on the ceiling. An identical device surveyed the bathroom. He wondered why the powers-that-be chose to monitor only those two rooms. It made little sense. He did nothing in his apartment that required such scrutiny—especially not in the bathroom of all places. He didn't even need to use it.

At that moment, a cockroach skittered on the ceiling above him.

Charles regarded the insect. His eyes reddened. The stench of sulfur filled the air. A moment later, tendrils of smoke seeped from the bug's body. It lost its grip on the plaster and fell to the floor—dead within seconds. He turned around and saw another roach crawling up the wall and made its legs fall off.

Charles felt a twinge of guilt for taking his aggression out on insects, but they were the only thing he was powerful enough to effect. Sometimes he could make a person turn around by staring at them, but even humans could do that.

He leaned over and turned off the lamp. Darkness enveloped him and, for the first time that day, he felt at peace.

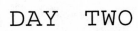

DAY TWO

CHARLES LAID IN bed for hours, enjoying that awake-but-not-awake sensation he could cultivate on days when the alarm didn't ring. At 2 P.M. he finally arose. Even then he didn't want to do anything, but when he went to the refrigerator and found it empty, he knew he'd have to go to the store. His stomach rumbled. He tried to remember the last time he'd eaten and thought that it might have been at *The Burger Hut* the day before.

The store closest to him—one of those everything-under-one-roof places—had once been a temple built by an ancient tribe with an unpronounceable name. There, shoppers trampled through halls that had once held the corpses of chieftains. Women bought glittery handbags on the same spot where young girls had been sacrificed so that a village might receive an abundance of rain. A year after his arrival, it had been transported, brick by brick, from its original location and rebuilt in the center of town. Then, it had been hollowed out and filled with track lighting, metal shelving, and pale beige floor tiles. It made Charles sick to see history defiled, even if it was human history, but necessity dictated patronage.

* * * *

A song played over the intercom as he entered the temple/store. He recognized it as a currently popular tune.

I'll see you in the grave,
The grave, grave, grave.
That's where you and I belong, baby.
Oh yeah.
That's where we neeeeeeeed to be.
Come on, sista-sweet
wrap your hands around my meat,
my bloaty-bloaty corpse meat
in the grrrraveeee.

And then the jazzy chorus kicked in:

We be fightin', killin', eatin'
—flowin' in time's jizz.
We be fightin', killin', eatin'
—flowin' in time's jizz.

    He tried to block out the rest, even covering his ears at one point, but still heard the song. It was as though the radio waves had bypassed his ears and beamed straight into his brain.

    The song went off, but a worse one took its place. Again, there was no tuning it out. Charles was forced to listen as he picked up what he needed, first in the dairy aisle and then in the breakfast aisle. He wanted more, but milk, eggs, yogurt, and cereal were the only things in the store that didn't consist of processed or reconstituted people. The big superstore across town had a larger selection of non-human items, but Charles didn't relish the hours-long walk to get to it. Demons weren't allowed on the subway.

    He reached for a box of *Flang-Os* and remembered the advertisement outside *The Burger Hut*. He cursed himself and reached for the *Shreddy-Puffs* instead. At that moment, someone stepped up behind him.

"Yo, yo, yo gator-slice! Home-cheese gotta little sumthin' fo' this bitchnitzitch?"

Charles tensed up. Human-on-demon violence was rare, but was it *Demon Day*? Panic welled up inside until he remembered that *Demon Day* wasn't until Friday.

He turned around and saw another young guy hopped up on Mexotrexic-8. They tended to be more annoying than threatening. Still, Charles remained wary. He tried his best to match the guy's dialect. "No, bitchnitzitch. I ain't got nothin' fo' yah."

"That's okay, 'cause I already be ridin' high, baby! Are yah ridin' high, too?"

"Yeah, I be ridin' high. Thanks for asking." Charles then grabbed the box of *Shreddy-Puffs* and walked off.

The kid screamed behind him. "Thanks fo' askin'? *Thanks fo' askin'!* What tha fuck yah flappin' about?"

He couldn't believe he'd been so stupid. Waxing polite around a Mexotrexic-8 tripper was the one thing that set them off.

The kid stalked up to Charles and got in his face. He opened his mouth. Charles recoiled at the smell, imagining decaying rodents pressed up against him.

"Who tha fuck sez 'Thanks fo' askin'?'" He leaned in even closer. "Yah ain't one-uh those pussy-snatzches, are yah?" Then he shrieked. "*I hate me sum pussy-snatzches!*"

Charles shook his head. It was preferable to talking.

"Well, if yah ain't a pussy-snatzch, then yah betta sez it rite!"

Charles' brain clattered. He had no idea what to say. He

hadn't studied the new urban dialects very closely, though he'd been told by *the Bureau of Demonic Immigration* that he should do so. But he had to say *something*, the kid was leaning closer and closer, his teeth moving up and down, like he wanted to chew off Charles' nose. "That's…uh…nice to hear, *yah fuckin' fuck*." He paused. "Uh…*Dat betta?*"

The kid leaned back. Charles couldn't read his face until a smile crossed it. "Yeah, my bitchnitzitch. Yah be kooleezaa."

"Well, yah be *kooleezaa*, too." He stepped backwards. The kid seemed appeased and didn't follow, though he did take an ultra-sized box of *Flang-Os*, open it, and empty the whole thing into his saggy pants. As he walked away, Charles heard crunching sounds.

He carried his groceries to one of the checkout lanes. A rack was positioned to the side of its entrance. A big overhead sign read IMPULSE BUYS. Suddenly, everything went black. The next thing he knew, he was standing in line, his arms loaded with items from the rack.

It took over a minute to return the stuff. When he looked back, someone had taken his place in line. The man, some city cowboy looking fellow, seemed to know the guy who was checking him out.

The employee looked down at a blender as he ran it over the sensor. "Looks like you've come to get your fix, my man."

The customer stroked his blue jean bulge. "Sure as shootin', Tommy."

"We got some nice new toasters back there, too. They put the last model to shame."

"They still got that—whatcha' call it—'user interface capacity'?"

The employee grinned. "They've got that and more."

Charles was repulsed, but had to listen. He felt the *Shreddy-Puffs* slip from his grasp so he held them tighter.

The employee leaned in closer to the cowboy. "Let me mention something that might interest you. Most tend to shy away from such things, but you look like a man who might appreciate the deep fryer."

"Sounds like I'd be a little hot to trot, afterwards. If yah know what I mean..."

"But it's worth it, man. Every penny."

They refused to stop talking. Fifteen minutes passed, and the line grew longer and longer. A few of the customers in the rear weren't taking the wait very well. Charles heard gurgling sounds behind him and assumed someone was getting throttled. He also heard a wet sucking and sloshing sound, which disturbed him too much to consider.

He moved quietly to another aisle where the line was much shorter, though he almost slipped in a red pool before he got there. In just under a minute, he stood before a dumpy, thirty-something woman whose teeth were more unruly than her hair. Her left ankle was tethered to a pole, so she couldn't move more than a foot to either side of the register.

"Hey there, cutie," she said. "Thanks for shopping with us today."

"No problem."

She seemed friendly enough, but Charles observed her putting stones in along with his groceries to make the bag heavier.

"That'll be $52.25."

He knew the actual total couldn't be more than $15, but paid anyway.

"Thanks, and please come back soon."

"I will."

She sneered. "Oh, go to hell."

Charles didn't comment on that, though he felt a sudden sense of loss in his gut that was as heavy as the stones in his bag.

He exited the store. Across from him, on the other side of the lot, a large black rock had jutted from the pavement, dislodging a whole parking space. It was sharp and shiny looking, like obsidian. He didn't recall seeing it when he walked in, and he didn't think he could miss something so strange and obvious. He wanted to walk over and touch it, but then the fire hoses outside the store came on, spraying Charles and other lingering ex-customers away.

* * * *

Charles opened the door to the stairwell and realized that his apartment had been broken into. He could see only the uppermost section of the door, but it was noticeably ajar, and he always locked up before leaving.

He walked up the stairs quietly, cursing the steps each time they let out a squeal. At the top, he paused. He drew in a few deep breaths and peered through the space between the facing and the door.

He saw Helen, the social worker who had been assigned to his case, sitting primly on the sofa. He sighed—the last thing he wanted to do was talk to her—before he realized how it would betray his presence. She spotted him. A large smile bloomed across her face.

"Oh Ralph, hello! Hope you don't mind that I let myself in."

"I would have preferred that you hadn't. And the name's

Charles."

"Sorry Tim, but we can't undo what's been done, now can we? Take a seat. I want to know how you've been doing. It's been two weeks since our last visit."

"Sure, whatever. But do you mind if I put my groceries up first?"

"Oh no, go right ahead. I won't move a muscle."

"Want anything to drink?" he called out. "I've got water and milk."

"No thank you, Steve. I'm fine."

Charles gritted his teeth.

In the kitchen, he sat the bags on the table. He got the groceries out first and then removed four sizable stones from the bottom of the bag.

Then he saw the bomb.

He rammed his hand into the bag and seized the bomb; no time to read the timer. He ripped off a red wire that connected dynamite to alarm clock and threw the whole thing into the sink, which he filled with water.

He'd dealt with bombs in grocery bags once before. That had been at his other apartment. He considered himself lucky that he had to run two defecating youths out of the yard just as the thing detonated. Demons healed quickly, but a small bomb blast would have probably left him maimed for months.

"What's going on in there?" Helen asked.

"Just a bomb in the grocery bag. I've got everything under control."

"Really? My sister got one of those last week. Blew her head clean off."

Charles had no idea how to respond, so he quietly put the groceries in the cabinet and fridge. Helen was stuffing something into her pocketbook upon his return. He didn't question her. Whatever she was stealing couldn't be that valuable or important. The only thing he really cared about was his laptop, and that was still safely on the coffee table.

"Now that's done," she said as Charles took his seat beside her, "you can tell me how the last two weeks have treated you."

He shrugged. "Well, I'm still employed, if that counts for anything."

"It does. It does. And are you still holding two jobs?"

"Yeah. At *The Burger Hut* and *Tony's Used Cars*."

"Enjoying them?"

A lie, he decided, was better than the truth. "Yes, immensely."

"Wonderful! It's important that new arrivals not only be productive citizens but also enjoy what they do. And it's even more important now that the new laws have been passed. You're aware of the new laws, aren't you?"

"I don't keep up with people politics."

"Father Malachi passed a couple just last week."

"I thought he was just an advisor. Isn't the leader that Grand Dictator II fellow?"

Helen waved her hand dismissively. "You really don't pay much attention, do you—anyway, the new law states that you can be thrown into a concentration camp for joblessness. You don't want that, do you?"

Charles shook his head.

"Of course you don't, but you know what they say about all work and no play." Helen farted discreetly into the cushion. "Now tell me, how do you spend your leisure time?"

"I sometimes check my email."

She made a tisk-tisk sound. "Grape City is a big place, Paul."

"I thought I told you the name's Charles."

"That's neither here nor there. The point is that there's plenty to do and see, so there's no excuse for sitting around like a lump."

"But there's nothing I want to do here. Honestly. No symphonies, no galleries— nothing like what I was used to in Hell. The only thing that's halfway decent about this city is the park."

"So, you go there often?"

"Not often, but when I do, I always make sure to feed the ducks."

"That's pretty lame. Have you ever hack-fucked?"

"No."

"Rape-slammed?"

"No."

Helen shook her head. "I know your kind tends to disapprove of the way we do things, but it's important that you embrace the culture of those you live amongst. Assimilation is paramount. You don't want to feel like an alien all your life, do you?"

Charles glared at her. "I'm a demon, not an alien."

She chuckled. "I was speaking metaphorically, but I'll have you know that I'm not big into all that stuff, either." She leaned in closer. "And to be honest, the only thing I've ever done is bang-raped. It's pretty mild, and I only did it because I saw that billboard over on 8th."

"Yeah, I see that billboard all the time, too. But I've never bang-raped."

"But you did torture the souls of the damned, didn't

37

you?"

"Yes, but that's different."

Helen draped an arm around him. "Is it really?"

Rage boiled. In his mind, Charles watched Helen simmer in a vat of semen and feces, her flesh sliding from bones as he stirred and stirred and stirred. He knocked her arm from his shoulder. "It sure as hell is different!"

She threw her hands up. "No need to get testy. I'm only trying to help."

He refused to listen. "And I'll tell you why it's different—because it had a reason and a purpose. That's *exactly* what separated our darkness from your stupid circus."

"Your defensiveness speaks volumes."

Now, Charles saw Helen being torn limb from limb by a pack of starving hellbeasts. The fantasy was going too far. He forced the thought from his mind and made himself calm down.

"But you've only bang-raped," he said. "That must mean a part of you doesn't feel comfortable, that just wishes to God—" Charles couldn't believe he'd said that word. He paused briefly to regain his bearings. "That just wishes it would all stop."

When she spoke, nearly ten seconds later, her voice sounded flat and perfunctory. "I have friends who hack-fuck and bang-rape and slam-kill, and I don't want to say anything bad about them."

"But—"

"No buts! Besides, I didn't come here to get into an argument. The real reason I came was to let you in on a surprise."

He went cold on the inside. "What surprise?"

"A night on the town. Trust me, it's just what the doctor ordered."

"I already told you—"

"No, no. You don't understand. I've set you up on a blind date."

"*A blind date*! Are you a social worker or a match-maker?"

"I admit it's not a normal part of the job, but I like to go the extra mile for my clients. Believe it or not, I care about you, Harold. Jeanine is a friend of my brother, and I picked her out just for you."

Charles gripped the cushion. "But how can you say you picked her out just for me when you can't even remember my name!"

"Don't worry. She's a homebody, too—but that doesn't mean she isn't a looker. I'm sure you'll love her if you just give her a chance. Can you do that for me, Roger?"

"*Charles*!"

"Can you, please?"

He exhaled. He dreaded going out with a human, but perhaps he could stomach it, provided she wasn't another foaming lunatic or indifferent lump. It might actually be nice to do something with someone else. At the very least, it would mean *change*.

Charles finally nodded.

"Is that a yes?"

He nodded again.

"Great! She embraced him in a hug. "I'll have the limo pick you up tomorrow after work."

"Limo?"

Helen beamed. "Yes, and you'll both be going to a very

nice restaurant. I won't tell you which, though. It'd spoil the surprise. And don't you worry about money, either. Everything's paid."

"I see."

"You're working at the used car lot until 5 tomorrow, right?"

"Right."

"Then I'll have the driver pick you up here at 6:30. Is that a good time?"

"As good as any, I guess."

She stood up and slung her purse over her arm. It banged against her hip and made a sloshing sound. "This is great news. You won't regret it, Frank. Trust me."

* * * *

Charles spent the next hour rummaging in his closet for something nice to wear. He figured that if he was going to bite the bullet, then he might as well look good biting it.

The only things he found that weren't threadbare or didn't have holes were his *Burger Hut* uniform and the suit that his boss at the used car dealership made him buy.

He hated the suit—it reminded him of what dead men wore when they went to meet worms—but he hated the uniform more.

The green clip-on he tried first didn't work with the suit. Charles reached into the dresser drawer and pulled out a handful of ties. He returned to the mirror and held each tie in front of his neck, one after the other.

He rather liked the one with the lobster pattern; it was amusing. Still, he didn't think his boss would approve. He also feared his date might find it too frivolous. Finally, he decided on a dark blue tie.

Charles took all these clothes and laid them across the sofa so they wouldn't be wrinkled in the morning.

* * * *

Later that night, he turned on the computer. He never intended to become a creature of habit, but, ever since he got the computer, he found it progressively harder to go a day without logging on.

He didn't check the displaced demon group—he figured there'd be no need—but went straight to his email instead. There were even more junk messages than usual, so many that he nearly deleted the only important message of the bunch.

An email from Satan.

He felt a rare sensation—an excited tingle that dissipated as soon as he read the first sentence.

Dear Charles,

I had to have Cerebus put to sleep today. I'm so sorry, Charles. I know you loved him, but there was nothing I could do. The landlord told me the dog had to go.

Really having a bad day. Wish this e-mail could be longer, but I don't feel like writing anymore.

Oh, and I have a job interview tomorrow. It's in telemarketing. Wish me luck, 'cause I need money more than anything else right about now.

Until next time,
Satan

Charles sank into the sofa. Cerebus—put to sleep. Cerebus—*dead*.

As a demonspawn, he'd chased that old hound across burning red landscapes and up the jagged peaks of Blackfuck Mountain, throwing the arms and legs of the damned for him to chase after and bring back. Cerebus would drop these severed limbs at Charles' feet and then look up, panting and begging for another round.

He couldn't think of a time without that dog. He'd sat beside him as he struggled through Minion School homework. Later, not a day passed that he didn't aid in Charles' wholesale torture of the damned. Charles so missed dishing out well-deserved torment. It was unfortunate that the flickering souls of the damned had been snuffed out when Hell closed shop.

He tried to lose himself in Hell-based memories that didn't, in some way, involve Cerebus. It was an impossible task. There'd been other dogs, sure, but Cerebus was the best of them all, even better than the dog that the humans liked so well, the one he'd seen on TV before TV stopped showing old family fare. Charles forgot the dog's name, and then recalled it—*Old Yeller.*

* * * *

In bed, Charles tossed and turned. The room felt hot and his covers sticky. He tried turning around and sleeping by the foot of the bed. That didn't work. Each time he neared sleep, he'd first think of Cerebus and then fret about his upcoming date. The cycle didn't end.

There was only one thing that would get him to sleep.

Charles arose and turned on the lamp. He retrieved a gallon bucket and a washcloth from beneath the bed.

Sometimes, he didn't want to do it anymore—it felt like his very essence was spurting from the tip of his penis—but sleeping pills had no effect on him. In Hell, he could have banged a Fire Maiden or two and then returned to bed, satisfied and ready for a good night's sleep. But Fire Maidens didn't exist anymore. They didn't react well to the Earth's atmosphere and, like the damned, were extinguished upon arrival.

Charles sat on the edge of the mattress, his penis inside the bucket. He stroked himself joylessly until an orange gout shot forth and filled the pail to brimming. Bringing the steaming mess to the bathroom, he flushed it down the toilet. Then he cleaned out the bucket so that it wouldn't be even more disgusting come morning.

Still, he didn't get to sleep until an hour before dawn.

DAY THREE

IN THE MORNING, after the alarm had blasted him from a short, troubled sleep, Charles stood naked before the mirror. His reflection appeared flabby and pale, the result of too much fried food and not enough exercise. The muscle definition he had sported in Hell was lost. He didn't imagine that it'd ever return.

He almost hoped his date would be another repulsive lunatic. If he liked her, and she liked him, then she'd surely wind up seeing him naked.

That would never do.

Charles covered himself as quickly as possible. He uttered a demonic chant under his breath as he left the bedroom on route to the stairwell. It was just for luck. Demonic chants didn't work in the world.

* * * *

An hour later, he stood in the middle of the used car dealership lot, watching customers smash windows, hotwire cars, and speed off in expensive convertibles. Not a single automobile had been sold in the month that he'd worked for *Tony's Used Cars*.

He heard a rumble and looked towards the sound. A tour bus with Canadian plates pulled in front of the lot. Its door opened, and a group of thirty ordinary looking people disembarked. Some held cans of spray-paint. Others held sledgehammers, blowtorches, or knives.

Tour group vandals—but at least they were better behaved than those who came off the street.

A 40-ish woman in a white blouse and skirt walked up to him. "Hi there. How's your day going, hon?"

"Not too bad, I guess."

She smiled and then turned to slash the tires of a station wagon.

Charles watched the melee, sometimes wincing at the sound of shattering glass and crumpling metal. If he was supposed to stop it, he hadn't been told. Tony never complained.

The whole affair lasted only a few minutes. At the end, as others returned to the bus, a man wearing pleated slacks and a button-up shirt patted him on the back. "Hey, thanks for the opportunity," he said. "This has been the best lot yet."

"Well, it isn't mine. It belongs to Tony." Charles pointed at the trailer in the center of the lot. "He's in there."

"Well, give him my regards. I've vandalized fifty lots thus far and not one has compared to *this*." He sighed. "But the tour ends tomorrow, then it's back to work."

"So, what do you do?"

"I'm an accountant for the *The Slutty Italian*. It's a pizza, spaghetti, and rape restaurant in Toronto."

"Oh."

"Well, thanks again!" And, with that, the man was back on the bus on his way to the next scheduled lot.

* * * *

As the day progressed, more and more cars were either vandalized or stolen. Another tour bus had pulled in just an hour and a half after the first departed. Then the street punks arrived, howling and screaming. Charles wished he had headphones. He'd play the B-52s CD he'd found and block out their mad monkey noises. By the time they'd finished, Charles counted twelve cars that hadn't been completely ruined.

He didn't relish talking with Tony, but figured he had little choice. His boss didn't mind the usual daily damage, but this was insane.

And so he walked to Tony's sky blue trailer, his feet crunching glass. A particularly sharp piece breached his shoe and entered his foot. It hurt, but the wound would heal in minutes. He pulled the fragment out and tried not to think anymore of it, even as the inside of his shoe began to feel slick.

He knocked on the door. A voice behind it: "Yeah?"

"Charles, here. I wondered if you might have a minute."

An exasperated grunt: "Stop talking through the door and come inside."

Charles entered the tiny office, a simple white room with indoor/outdoor carpeting, bookshelf, and desk. His boss sat behind the desk, shirtless and smoking a fat cigar. Charles guessed his weight at about three hundred pounds.

"Forgive me, but I thought today's property loss might concern you."

Tony laughed, but it dissolved quickly into a series of dry, hacking coughs. It took a moment before he recovered enough to speak. When he did, his voice was harsh, raspy, and grating. "I *am* concerned, but not in the way you think. I don't get money for selling cars. It's the tour groups that keep me in the black. They pay a healthy fee for the honor of vandalizing my fine autos. It's more than enough to make up for anything that's stolen or bashed by fuckin' street punks."

"I had no idea."

"I don't pay you to know things. An employee who knows is a bad employee. You're not a bad employee, are you Charles?"

He shook his head.

"I didn't think you were." Tony leaned forward in his seat. "In fact, I've been watching you, and I'm impressed. Past employees just hack-raped or bang-murdered the tourists on sight. That was bad for business, so I had to hack-rape or bang-murder them back—according to gender, mind you. But you've been here a month and I haven't had to bang-murder you yet." He smiled, showing big yellow teeth. "That's a new record."

"I'm honored, I guess."

"And you should be. Otherwise, you'd become part of my *collection*."

"I understand, sir."

"Do you want to see it? My collection, I mean. You're a good employee; I'd trust you in my basement."

"I really can't. I've got to do something right after work."

"Are you sure?"

"Yes. Very. Extremely."

"Well, maybe some other time'll be better." Tony sat back in his seat. The leather beneath him squealed. "But get back to work now, Charles. Do me proud."

* * * *

Charles did Tony proud for five additional hours. By that time, the twelve untouched autos were down to three.

It was the most lucrative day in the history of *Tony's Used*

Cars. Charles wondered if he'd get a raise, but doubted it.

* * * *

At home, he paced the floor, biting his nails and spitting them—slime-coated—to the floor.

His brow felt sweaty. Charles got a washcloth and quickly wiped away green perspiration. He imagined it wouldn't make for a good first impression.

He looked at the clock: 6:15.

Grabbing a clean washcloth, he buffed his metallic facial pins. He was surprised at how tarnished and dull they'd become. He'd never had to buff them once in Hell. Then he stood in front of the mirror for a while, trying to will away love handles. He didn't expect it to work, and it didn't.

Charles left the bathroom and walked to the window that faced the street. He raised the blinds and watched a few people walk up to the building and then disappear into *The Machine Shop*. A black car entered his line of sight. He felt a surge of both dread and excitement, but it was only a hearse. Finally, after three minutes spent staring at the window, a long black limousine pulled up in front of his apartment.

A knot formed in Charles' stomach. Before he left, he had to draw in a deep breath and close his eyes for a few seconds.

Outside, the limousine idled. Its driver already held open one of the many passenger-side doors for him.

"Step right in, sir," he said. Charles noted a long string of gristle hanging over his bottom lip, but didn't mention it.

Charles wasn't all that eager to get into a car driven by another person—it generally wasn't the safest thing—but the simple fact that the limousine had gotten to his place in one piece and with no obvious blood spatters on the grille did much to boost his confidence.

He ducked into the limo and saw a woman sitting in the seat across from him.

Jeanine.

He froze. He'd expected that they'd pick her up next, that he'd have some time to collect himself. The knot in his stomach became a boulder.

She smiled. Her teeth were straight and clean. "Hello, there Randy."

"C-Charles," he stammered. "Name's Charles."

Her voice was pleasant. "Oh, really? Helen told me your name was Randy."

"I'm, uh, not surprised." He took his seat beside her and scrunched his hands together in his lap, forcing himself to not rock back and forth. "She's not, uh, good with names."

"Tell me about it. I've known her for eight years, and she's called me every name in the book. Once, she called me Pete."

Charles laughed. The boulder in his stomach once again became a knot, but this time it was smaller. "She hasn't called me a woman's name yet, but I guess it's only a matter of time."

"She means well, but it gets annoying."

He nodded. Charles was surprised at the ease with which the conversation was flowing. He was also surprised at how pretty Jeanine was. He'd grown accustomed to repulsive, dirty, smelly, and misshapen people, but she wasn't repulsive, dirty, smelly, or misshapen at all. She didn't even have a cold sore. Her skin looked soft and smooth. Her light brown hair was long and straight and complimented her skin nicely. He guessed she might be in her early thirties, but didn't dare ask. Charles looked down at her clothes—a skirt and blouse, simple yet elegant. He caught himself staring too long at her bosom and turned away quickly.

"What's wrong?"

The car bounced as the driver took out a pedestrian. "I uh, I uh, uh…"

"You're shy, aren't you? I find that sweet."

He turned to her again, making sure that he looked no further south than her eyes. "You do?"

"Sure. I'd scream if I had to deal with another Casanova."

"Well I'm not that type, Jeanine. Do you mind if I call you Jeanine?"

"Of course not, silly. It's my name." She rifled through her purse. Charles cringed, imagining she'd pull out something hideous. Instead, she removed a compact, opened it, and checked her makeup. So," she said as she dabbed blush on her cheeks, "do you know where we're going? Helen didn't tell me anything."

"She didn't tell me anything either."

The limousine hit another organic bump. "Oh well, I guess we'll find out when we get there. I just hope we don't go to *Café Homme*. I can't stand those cannibal places, even the ritzy ones."

A non-cannibal, Charles was relieved. "Yeah," he replied. "I don't much go for people, either."

* * * *

Ten minutes later, the limousine pulled into the parking lot of *The Swinging Lantern*, one of Grape City's trendi-est downtown bistros. The last few minutes of the drive had been awkward. The driver had taken to driving on the side-walk. Once, Jeanine had been forced up from her seat when the limo drove over a newspaper dispenser. She landed in Charles' lap. He was surprised when this happened, and even more surprised to feel himself get hard.

He prayed Jeanine hadn't noticed.

Charles jumped when the door opened, but it was just the driver, there to escort them out.

"Enjoy your meal," he said, the gristle string flapping against his chin.

* * * *

The Swinging Lantern would have been a quaint little tavern if it weren't for all the people smacking their food. Some didn't even use silverware, or their hands. A young couple in the far right corner was the worst. They chewed their food and then regurgitated into each other's mouths, like birds. The collective sight and sound was grating, and it was only Jeanine's presence that kept his teeth from clenching.

They took a booth that was as far removed from the other customers as possible. From that vantage point he couldn't see them—the seat backs were too high—but he could still hear their chomps and slurps.

The waiter arrived seconds later.

"Hello, my name is Billy. Our special today is kidney stuffed pancreas, sizzled in freshly squeezed man-seed and served with a side of rice pilaf. If you're looking for a more casual evening, the flesh puffs are on special today, too. Filled with aged gorgonzola cheese and smegma, they're deep fried to perfection."

"No thanks," Jeanine said." I'll have the Squid King Alaska, extra rare."

"An excellent choice." The waiter turned to Charles. "And what can I get you, sir?"

He glanced down at his menu. "Uh, the house salad, I guess. But can I get it without testicles?"

The waiter frowned. "But our testicles are always extra juicy. We harvest them fresh in the kitchen."

"Okay, okay. I'll just pick them off."

"And don't forget to bring us a bottle of your best wine." Jeanine leaned forward. "You drink wine, don't you?"

"I've tried it once or twice."

"Okay, so that's one Squid King Alaska, extra rare, one house salad and a bottle of our finest wine, right?"

Charles and Jeanine nodded at the same time. The waiter took their menus, said his thanks, and then disappeared into the kitchen. Seconds later, Charles hear piercing shrieks. It was, he assumed, the sound of his unwanted salad topping being harvested.

"This is one of my favorite restaurants," she said over and above the din. "I'm glad Helen chose it for us."

"And picked up the tab," Charles added.

Jeanine smiled. "Hey, you're witty, too!"

He blushed. He didn't know he was capable of blushing.

* * * *

Fifteen minutes passed, and the waiter returned with

their food. Charles noticed the spreading red stain on the crotch of his khakis.

"Sorry for taking so long," he said, "we ran low on testicles, so the chef had to improvise in the kitchen."

"But I didn't even want balls!"

"One taste will change your mind."

Charles grimaced. He looked from the waiter to the dishes he carried. The Squid King Alaska was eldritch-looking and unspeakable. His salad didn't look bad, though, aside from the ball-topping, eight to ten balls it seemed.

The waiter placed their food in front of them. He motioned again towards the kitchen, but collapsed before he got halfway there.

* * * *

"Do you like your Squid King Alaska?"

"It's sensational. The best I've ever had."

He concentrated on her eyes each time she brought a bite to her mouth. She was so nice and pretty; it hurt to see her consume such ghastly stuff. At least she used silverware and chewed with her mouth closed.

"Well, I'll have to try it next time I come."

"I'll give you some of mine, if you'd like."

"No, no thanks." He paused for a moment. "I'm on a diet."

"A diet, oh come on. You don't need to diet."

"I don't?"

"You look fine, Charles. "

"You don't think I look like a fat freak?"

"Of course not. I love your look, especially the face-things. Did it hurt to get them?"

"No, I was born with them."

"Really? That's fascinating." She reached out and touched a pin-tip. "So sharp."

"Well, I *did* have the sharpest face pins in Hell."

She took a bite of what appeared to be a gelatinous green tentacle. "You must have been a really important guy down there."

"I was the highest-ranking minion in the Ninth Circle, but it really wasn't down, you know. It had its own dimension."

"Sorry. I bet you hate it when people get that wrong."

Charles nibbled on his salad. "Not really. I'm used to it."

* * * *

Charles fidgeted with his napkin as dinner reached its end. He wanted to tell Jeanine how he felt, but he didn't want to come across as stupid or put his foot in his mouth by saying too much. The knot in his stomach returned, as, finally, he let the words fly.

"I'd love to get to know you better, Jeanine," he said. "I honestly thought this date would be a total disaster, but I've never had a better time on Earth. And I mean that, too. I'm not just throwing you a line."

"And I'd like to get to know you better, Charles."

He wanted to reach across the table and embrace her. "I had such a low opinion of humanity before I met you. I guess I should have never grouped all of you together. Thanks for showing me my mistake, Jeanine. I appreciate it more than you know."

"No problem, Charles, but could you excuse me for a second? I've got to go to the little girl's room."

"Not a problem. I'll wait." He almost added 'all night if I have to', but decided that would sound cheesy.

* * * *

With Jeanine gone there was no buffer between him and the other people in the restaurant. The gnashing sounds grew louder and louder. Charles turned to one of the big screen TVs on the wall. He didn't care what was on it. He just wanted to lose himself in *something* until she returned.

The TV was tuned to the all-politics channel. On screen, Father Malachi—advisor to the Grand Dictator II—stood behind a podium alongside the sickly and ineffectual looking leader. Human politics left a bad taste in his mouth, which meant he rarely followed it. Still, he knew that the two men had ascended to power on Earth the same day that Hell closed its doors. He found that odd, and it didn't help that Malachi—a tall guy with ashen skin and a prominent widow's peak—had a strange presence about him, something that was tangible yet indescribable. In the past, he could have looked into the man's future and saw his destiny, but that power was gone, too.

He could barely hear Malachi's speech over the din. *"horrible—transformations—in cities—then the rest of— later—a few more years—all your kind has left to—omni- virus—super-plague—syphilis—your pills to swallow— yourselves to blame—job is done—take my leave of you now."*

The Grand Dictator II then moved forward to speak. In

the background, Father Malachi made a beaconing motion with his hands. A group of armed men burst into the chamber the moment the leader stopped speaking. After a short go around, they slaughtered at least a half dozen people, including the Grand Dictator II.

Father Malachi disappeared in a cloud of smoke and fire.

Charles turned from the TV and looked around the restaurant. No one seemed to notice or care.

When Jeanine returned a few minutes later, he breathed an audible sigh of relief.

"Well, I feel a lot fresher now. Just took the biggest dump of my life."

He nearly choked on his last bite of lettuce. "Excuse me?"

"I hope no one goes in there for a few hours." She took her seat and plucked one of the testicles from Charles' plate. Then she popped it in her mouth. "Ummmm...*balls*."

He shrieked. "What did you just do?"

"No need to yell. I didn't think you wanted it."

"I didn't!"

"Then why are you upset?"

"Because you ate balls!"

"Yeah, so?"

"You told me you didn't eat people!"

She touched the half-eaten ball to his lips. "Come on, have a bite. It's got my spit all over it."

"No, please. No."

"Whatever." Jeanie dropped the ball to the floor where it hit with a splat. "Let's blow this joint so you can bang-rape me. Your place or mine?"

"What!"

"Okay then, I'll bang-rape you first."

"No, no, no!"

"Don't tell me you don't bang-rape on a first date."

Charles felt on the verge of blubbering. "I don't bang-rape at all." His face flushed. *"And you don't either!"*

She waved her hand dismissively. "Oh come on, I was just playing coy. It's what girls do. But you were just playing, too, right?"

"Of course not!" Charles felt his heart sink. "I *loved* you!"

"You're really like this. You aren't just playing games." She rolled her eyes.

"I'm not playing games at all! I don't even know how to play them!"

"Good God, I should have known that Helen would set me up with the likes of you." She threw her napkin on the table. "That *bitch*."

"Please don't—"

Words died. For a moment, it appeared as though her teeth had lengthened into razor-sharp points. He'd seen her teeth before, and they'd been straight and perfect, not cosmetically filed like Manager Jim's.

He thought he'd imagined the transformation. Then her teeth did it again.

Charles bolted from his seat. "I—I gotta go. *Now.*"

"Go then." She sneered, her teeth now straight. "I'll just bang-rape a big-cocked waiter—*right here on the table!*"

He barely heard her final words. He was already halfway across the restaurant. Before he exited, he glanced back towards the booth.

Jeanine was still there. Already, she had pulled one of the young waiters into the seat with her. She ripped off his trousers, pulled down his underpants, and shoved his ass full of silverware.

Charles could take no more. He ran through the door and almost banged into a large black rock that had shot up through the sidewalk. He was too shaken to be curious. He ran to the limo, relieved to see the driver outside, waiting. The thought of getting back in the car wasn't one he particularly relished, but he wanted to be away from the restaurant as quickly as possible.

"Where's your date, sir?" The driver asked, the gristle now gone. "I assumed she'd come out with you."

"Uh, I horror-rape slammed her."

His eyes lit up. "Hey, hey, a combo! Good goin' my man!" Then the limo driver raised his hand like he wanted a high-five. Charles obliged him, and, during the high-five, the driver tickled his palm.

Charles felt diseased.

Once in the car, he braced himself for another round of pummeling. It didn't take long before the first pedestrian—homeless, from the looks of him—found his way beneath the limo's wheels.

The man rolled down the window that isolated the driver's compartment. "I take it that you want to go back to your place."

"No, take me to the park."

* * * *

The limo sped away into the night, leaving Charles alone

at park's edge. There weren't many people out, partly because it was late, and partly because the wind was blowing hard. It blustered against crotches and cold sores and spread disease even faster. In the past, people didn't mind as much. But viruses were becoming increasingly virulent.

Charles blessed the wind.

He entered the park and kept walking until he reached its center. He was so far from the road that he could barely hear the passing cars. The wind whistling through the oaks and willows was soothing. Charles was immune to sexually transmitted diseases, so he could concentrate on the sound's Zenlike qualities. Admittedly, the place was nothing like the grand parks of hell with their ever-flaming trees, molten pits, and sharp, crimson grass, but, at the moment, it was exactly the place he needed to be.

The only thing he didn't like was *The Children's Cauldron*—a place for the kiddies—but it was on the other side of the park. Behind its electric fence were strange contraptions and industrial-sized steel vats. He used to visit the park in the day, but then could hear sounds from *The Children's Cauldron*. Now, he never came before 5:00, when the cauldron closed.

He thought of Jeanine, about how she'd betrayed him, and about the inexplicable things that had happened to her teeth. He tried to force them from his mind. Such things didn't belong in a place of serenity.

But serenity couldn't seep in until he'd pounded his hands against his hips for nearly a minute. He only stopped once he heard the sound of ducks quacking behind him.

Rage subsided; Charles chuckled. The sound was amusing, and there was nothing quite like it in Hell. And the ducks themselves, so cute with their beady black eyes and orange webbed feet. They were his favorite of the Earth's creatures.

A dispenser had been placed to one side of the bench. It looked like something that might carry gumballs, but this one held croutons. *50 cents*, the sticker said.

In his pockets, he found exactly fifty cents. He went over to the machine and filled it with the change. He turned the crank, and a double handful of croutons fell from the slot.

Charles carried them over to the small pond where the ducks swam. He liked the setting sun and how it played on the water, and liked the ripples created by paddling duck feet. He felt more at peace than he had in months.

"Here duckie, duckie, duckie."

He'd hoped that one or more might waddle up close, but all stayed in the pond.

Charles threw some of the food their way, but they seemed as interested in food as they were in him. Instead, they attacked one another, disembodied bills and flying feathers in the air.

It was a duck geyser.

DAY FOUR

SATAN DIDN'T GET the telemarketing job.

Dear Charles,

"We are in the business of customer service. Who would want to pick up a phone and hear your voice?"—can you believe they said that?

I don't know what to do, Charles. I even thought about participating in Demon Day tomorrow. It'll hurt, I know—physically, mentally, and spiritually—but I'd be paid well, and I could sure use the money right now. If I don't get a grand soon my ass'll be on the streets. Damn it, I put Cerebus to sleep for this fucking place, so I'm not going to lose it. I'm willing to do whatever it takes. (But hey, if I do participate maybe I can stop by your place for a while.) :)

It almost hurt to make that smiley face. I never imagined it would come to this. Really, I never thought I could sink so low.

Come on, Charles. Write me a nice, happy email full of smiley faces. Tell me about all the good things that are happening to you right now.

Please.

— Satan

Charles wanted desperately to reply, but had nothing

to say. The truth would only depress Satan more. A lie would be a paper-thin charade, and Satan couldn't be fooled.

He put away the computer. In the bedroom, he forced himself into his uniform.

* * * *

The Burger Hut was in flames when Charles reached it. He'd never seen Manager Jim quite so happy.

"Charles, my sweet!" He twirled and sashayed just outside the building, naked, his body painted with strange runes and symbols. His manager's uniform lay crumpled in a heap on the ground. "So glad you made it!"

Charles stared agape at the structure, watching his job go up in flames.

"Yes, it's quite wonderful, isn't it? I had a vision last night. My true calling was laid out in series of colorful pie charts and diagrams. It was like a divine management training session, I tell you!"

Charles gestured to *The Burger Hut*, now fully engulfed. "But that doesn't explain this!"

"Oh it does, my little chickadee, it does! The whiteman told me I was wasting my life at *The Burger Hut*, that I'd never amount to anything if I stayed there. Then he revealed the path that I was to take. Wanna know that path?"

Charles didn't, but said 'yes' anyway.

"To be an actor in snuff films."

"*Snuff films?*"

"Sounds sexy, doesn't it?" Manager Jim batted his lashes. "I could put a good word in for you with the directors. I've always found you strangely attractive. I think it's your complexion, so *exotic*."

Charles ignored the last part of his answer. "Wait, that means you die on camera, right?"

"Yes, but I'm not worried. It's my destiny to be the only actor to appear in *multiple* snuff films. The white-man told me *that* was my special power, my calling. That's why I had to burn down the restaurant. It was a symbol of my old life, and had to be destroyed."

"But what about my co-workers? And the customers?"

"Oh, they won't cause any problems. I trussed them up and put them in the back. They were necessary sacrifices. The white-man said I couldn't gain the powers that were rightfully mine until I had cleansed everyone in *The Burger Hut* today, cleansed them with fire."

At that moment, the door swung open and two people ran, flaming, into the street.

"Hmmmm, guess I didn't tie a few of them tight enough. Oh well…"

* * * *

Charles spent the next few hours wandering about the town, looking for HELP WANTED or ENQUIRE WITHIN signs.

He wanted nothing more than to go back to his apartment, but figured that he might as well go on a job hunt since he was out. If he waited too long he feared he might wind up in a concentration camp or working in snuff films before the year was through. His life felt ready for meltdown—the bad date, the death of Cerebus, the loss of his job, *everything*. Things had to change, and finding a job that he could halfway enjoy would be a step in the right direction.

He noticed a few businesses with HELP WANTED signs, but gave each of them a wide berth. He had no interest in working in a butcher's shop or as a product tester. One involved killing with large knives and the other involved being killed by previously untested consumer items.

Charles was in the mood for neither.

Almost halfway across town, he passed an old brownstone that had been converted into business space. The sign above the door read SYSTILAC DATA PROCESSING. Directly below that, another HELP WANTED sign.

He wasn't sure what DATA PROCESSING implied, but, at the very least, it sounded more promising than the last two places he'd passed.

Charles walked up the steps and pulled open a heavy door. The room beyond was stark, white, and glaring. He shielded his eyes until they were able to adjust.

Apart from the receptionist desk—which was also white—the room was filled with large metallic cubes. Though they appeared to have no entrance, he heard the sound of clacking keys from within. A cannon also sat atop a marble base in the middle of the room.

At that moment, a group of suit-clad men entered from a sliding metal door to the left of the receptionist's desk. They looked determined as they walked up to one of the silver cubes. The man in front pointed a remote control at it. The cube grumbled and—though Charles saw no wires or pulleys—it rose to the ceiling, revealing an emaciated man hunched over a computer desk.

"Yes, that's the one."

The worker looked up, eyes wide. "No! No! I'm working! Can't you see that I'm working?"

"Your productivity has been down for two straight weeks, John."

"Just give me another week!" He pleaded. "I'd do better if you'd just give me my insulin! I promise!"

"We gave you a reprieve last week." Two men seized the worker, each grabbing hold of an arm. "And it's not company policy to dole out third chances, or insulin."

They dragged him, kicking and screaming, to the center of the room. There, the first man stuffed him inside the cannon, using a large stick to pack him in tighter. Another removed a book of matches from his coat pocket while adjusting the firing angle. A third hit a button on the remote. Each cube lifted simultaneously, revealing equally emaciated men and women. They turned towards the cannon—eyes blank and emotionless—as a fourth man took the matches from the second and lit the fuse.

Charles covered his ears just before the cannon exploded. The employee exited in a blur, his body spinning head over heels until it impacted against the wall to the right of a HANG IN THERE poster. A large bone fragment embedded itself just above the poster-kitten's claws.

Once the other employees had gotten a sufficient eyeful, the metal boxes descended and locked into place with a *click*. The typing sounds resumed immediately.

Charles stood motionless, watching shards of employee slide from the wall as the suit-clad men congratulated themselves and patted each other on the back. Then he walked over to the receptionist, an old gray-haired lady who wore glasses with a pearl string. He didn't much want the job after seeing what he'd seen, but he was a demon, and demons were hard to kill, even with cannons.

He stood beside the woman for almost a minute, listening to her crotch buzz as she looked over paperwork. He had no idea why her crotch was buzzing. If there was some electric pleasure-device down there, she didn't show it. Her face spoke more of constipation than bliss.

"Uh, hi."

The receptionist looked up. "Hi, yourself." Then she returned to her paperwork.

"I'm here to put in an application," he said, "but could you tell me what just happened?"

"Whatever the fuck do you mean, sir?"

"Well, uh." Charles gestured to the employee-covered wall.

"It's Thursday."

"I already knew that."

The receptionist glared. "Thursdays are Cannon Days. Cannon Days are good for productivity, and productivity is important to Mr. Mackelbaum."

"Mackelbaum?"

"My boss," she handed him an application, fifteen to twenty pages at least. "And your boss, too—if you're hired, and I hope to God that you're not." She harrumphed. "Sideshow reject."

"Oh, okay. Thanks, I guess." Charles bent over and began filling out the application.

The receptionist smacked his hand away. "Not on my desk, you idiot!" She pointed to a room across the hall. "Go there, fill out the application, and drop it in the slot provided. Wait five minutes before entering Mr. Mackelbaum's office— but don't forget to knock first! Is that clear?"

He nodded.

"Then go." She made a shooing motion with her hand.

Charles turned away and walked down the hall. It was also white, so white that it was hard to tell where the floor ended and the walls began. He was relieved to find that the room where he'd been sent wasn't white, but beige. It was also tiny and windowless. The only things inside it were a card table and a folding chair, both of which sat atop a rug.

He walked over to the chair. He'd almost sat down before he noticed the large, vibrating dildo that had been grafted to the middle of the seat. He looked at it askance, though it did explain why the secretary's crotch buzzed...

He avoided the chair and sat on his knees by the card table, leafing through the application, distressed at the number of questions, many of which were unnerving:

WHAT KIND/COLOR OF UNDERWEAR ARE YOU WEARING NOW?

DO YOU KNOW HOW TO POLE-DANCE?

PLEASE LIST NAMES AND ADDRESSES OF YOUR NEXT-OF-KIN.

Others seemed totally nonsensical.

IN 1,000 WORDS OR MORE PLEASE DESCRIBE YOUR LEFT INDEX FINGER.

ARE YOU?
"BLUE-GREEN DANCE, HA HA!" AGREE OR DIS-

AGREE WITH THIS STATEMENT?

Charles answered them to the best of his ability.

Hours passed. His hand felt like it was becoming an arthritic claw. He tried rubbing it, but that just made the pain in his knuckles dig deeper. Charles felt ten pounds lighter once the final blank had been filled.

He looked for the slot the receptionist said would be there, desperate to jettison the application. He saw nothing. Finally, after searching the entire room, he found the slot hiding beneath the rug. Still, he had to struggle with it for a few minutes before the stubborn flap opened.

Charles closed the flap and what sounded like a vacuum turned on inside. When he opened it again, the application was gone.

He spent the next five minutes sitting in a semi-lotus position on the floor, staring at the ceiling and listening to the gentle vibrations of the dildo on the chair.

* * * *

Five minutes later, he stood outside the office of Mr. Mackelbaum. The door was parted slightly, so he peered inside.

The boss—a thin, middle-aged man with a large bald spot—sat behind a mahogany desk. He looked disinterested as a guy danced around his office in skimpy blue briefs. The dancer still wore his employee nametag, only it was now pinned to his underwear. It identified him as MIKE.

"Drop 'em," Mr. Mackelbaum said while filing his nails.

"But—"

"I said drop 'em. You know the rules…"

The man dropped 'em. His dance became increasing provocative—hips pounding, ass shaking, penis flapping—but Mr. Mackelbaum continued to dote on his nails.

Charles opened the door wider. "Mr. Mackelbaum, sir." Then he remembered that he'd forgotten to knock.

"What!" Mr. Mackelbaum slammed the nail file on his desk. "Can't you see I'm in the middle of something **impor-** tant?"

"I'm sorry. I could come back later."

Mr. Mackelbaum exhaled noisily. "No, now's fine." Then he turned to the dancer. "Okay, Mike. You can go."

"Can I put my clothes on first?"

Mr. Mackelbaum threw his shirt at him. "Produce fifteen pages of output before the end of the day and you'll get your pants back. Otherwise, I'll burn them."

"But that's my last pair!"

"I know."

Charles stepped aside so that the man could leave the office. Once the door closed, Mr. Mackelbaum gestured with a forward sweep of his hands. "Take a seat," he said.

Charles walked over to the chair facing the desk. A vibrating dildo had been grafted onto it as well, though Mr. Mackelbaum's private area didn't seem to buzz.

He looked at Charles disapprovingly. "You didn't sit on the dildo. Not good, not good."

"I'm, uh, sorry about that. And I'm sorry for interrupting you in the middle of that guy's dance." It struck him that he'd apologized twice before the interview could even start. Surely a bad sign…

"Don't worry about interrupting the dance. It didn't do

anything for me. I'm not gay, but a man with my salary is required to have employees dance nude in front of him." Mr. Mackelbaum pointed his finger at Charles. "Worry about not sitting on the dildo."

"I—I'll do it next time. I think."

Mr. Mackelbaum leaned back. "Now what did you want, Mr.—"

"Charles."

"Yes, Mr. Charles. What can I do for you?"

"Well, I was wondering if you'd had time to look over my application."

"Application?"

"Yes, exactly."

"What application?"

"The one I just sent you."

"I received no application."

"It must be hung up in the pipes, because I put it where your receptionist told me to, in the slot."

"The vacuum system works flawlessly."

"Then you simply must have it!"

"Sorry, no applications have come through today." Mr. Mackelbaum resumed filing his nails.

"But that can't be—"

Then Charles noted the trashcan. An application sat atop piles of other applications. He recognized his own handwriting.

"You put my application in the trash!"

Mr. Mackelbaum was nonplused. "No, I didn't."

"Yes, you did!"

"I really must insist that I didn't."

"But I see it sticking out of the trashcan!"

He held out his left hand for Charles to see. "Think my cuticles look even?"

"I couldn't care less about your damn cuticles! I want to know why my application's been trashed!"

"It hasn't been. Your eyes are playing tricks on you." He paused to study his nails. "Do you think this one's a bit long?"

Charles ignored him. He fished his application from the trash and held it up to Mr. Mackelbaum's face. "See this! *My application*!"

"I don't see anything."

"How can you not see it? It's right in front of you!"

Mr. Mackelbaum leaned in closer. "Well, do I see something, now that you mention it."

"Good, because I was just about to—"

"An annoying and quite possibly mentally ill creature. That's what I see."

"Mental illness is unheard of in the demonic realm! It's your kind that's crazy!"

Mr. Mackelbaum sighed. "Even if I had your application—which I clearly do not—I wouldn't hire you. We don't hire people with body modifications. They might scrape the cannon barrel. It's an antique, you know."

Charles face flushed. "These aren't body modifications!"

"And your suit, did you get it at a thrift store? Come on now, Mr.—"

"Charles."

"Mr. Charles. Clothes are important because they reflect what's inside. By looking at your clothes, I'd say that you're akin to meat that's sat too long in the sun. Who'd want to hire spoiled meat? Not I, certainly."

"What's that supposed to mean?"

"And you're getting a little tubby. Letting yourself go, eh? Just sitting around the house, stuffing your face full of lard?"

"I hardly think my weight is an appropriate subject!"

"I beg to differ, Mr. Charles. Weight is *vitally* important in this or any job in which you must deal with a man of my caliber. I'd hate to see you dancing around here naked. I'd surely throw up."

Charles' mind flashed once again to images of pain and torture. He saw Mr. Mackelbaum's still-living head impaled on a stake. Demon dogs ate at him as he tried, and failed, to scream. He forced anger down and addressed Mr. Mackelbaum through clenched teeth.

"Can we cut the insults and get on with the interview?"

Mr. Mackelbaum spent a moment in thought. "I rather enjoyed insulting you. In fact, I'd love to continue doing it, but I'm a busy man with real-world things that require my attention. I have little time to deal with you and your fantasies, amusing though they may be."

"You're not going to interview me after I spent *four hours* with your stupid application!"

Mr. Mackelbaum laced his finger. "That is correct."

Charles stared at Mr. Mackelbaum's fingers. They stopped almost an inch past his wrists. They hadn't seemed so long earlier.

Just then, the door opened. Charles heard a young woman's voice behind him. "A call for you, Mr. Mackelbaum."

"I'll take it later." He resumed filing nails atop impossibly long fingers. "Busy."

"But the man on the other end says it's important."

Charles could hear only heavy breathing coming from the phone the secretary held.

"Oh, and hello." She giggled. "Didn't see you there for a moment."

He shot up in his seat. She'd sounded so similar to Jeanine. He turned to get a good look at the secretary. It wasn't last night's date, which was a relief. But relief vanished as soon as he noticed the woman's solid orange eyes.

Contacts! His mind screamed. *Just contacts*!

She smiled at him and winked like she was in on something that Charles wasn't. When she opened her mouth, a long, bi-forked tongue snaked out. He'd seen people who'd altered their tongues via surgery, but this looked *natural*.

He jumped from his seat and made for the door. The secretary stood in front of it. "Where are you going?"

He babbled.

"Don't leave. There's nothing to worry about." She smiled. "It'll all be over soon."

The last thing he wanted to do was stay. He brushed past her and ran down the hall and into the main workspace. He chanced a look over his shoulder. The secretary stared at him, half in and half out of Mr. Mackelbaum's office. She had a concerned expression and features that, from a distance, appeared normal.

Turning back around, he noticed that the cannon had been tipped over by another large black rock that had shot up through the floor, but Charles didn't pause to investigate. He bolted out the door and didn't stop running until he was five blocks removed from the SYSTILAC building.

* * * *

The people on the streets of Grape City appeared to have gone even crazier during the hours he'd spent inside SYSTILAC. In the past, he'd seen others walking down the street, behaving normally. He knew that they were probably going to—or leaving from—a bang-rape or a horror-kill. Either that, or they were too indifferent to engage in either. Still, in that single moment during which they passed, all appeared well.

Now, everyone and everything was on full display: rape-banging, fuck-murdering, horror-slamming, bang-killing, slam-fuck banging, murder-slam raping, horror-fuck killing, rape-bang slamming, even strange combinations for which Charles couldn't find words. Strangely, the victims seemed to enjoy what was happening to them—eyes rolled up in ecstasy, nipples erect, and bulges in their blood-soaked pants...

He ran quicker, sideswiping a woman who had sliced off her breasts to wear as twin hats. Across the street, one man was trying to climb into another man, orally. From the looks of it, he was almost a quarter of the way inside. Further ahead, a group of sixteen or more people poured from various cardboard boxes lining the street. He smelled trouble, and their collective body stench, from nearly a block away.

He looked around, but there was no side street into which he could duck.

The homeless soon encircled him.

"*Geblab blahge gehahablab*," they said collectively.

He'd heard the weird language of the homeless before, but never had it sounded so high-pitched and sonic.

"Please go away. I don't have spare change."

They didn't listen. Hungry faces pressed up against him, a sea of flapping lips and repulsion.

"*Coo-nama effenkata hoffenpoopa.*"

"I'm—I'm sorry." He tried to walk through, but the circle grew tighter. "I—I don't understand you."

"*Hardefleganharhar?*" They inquired, again in unison, as they picked at Charles' facial pins. "*Boohanoogla?*"

He smacked hands away, but more arose—touching, probing. He felt on the verge of drowning.

"Leave me alone!"

That only agitated them. "*Tatayakamataula!*" They screamed, yellow spit flying in Charles' face. "*Tatayakamataula! Tatayakamataula!*"

"Please, I'll give you money tomorrow if you just let me go today!"

"*Zoosootia! Zootsootia! Zootsootia!*"

Their voices became higher and higher pitched each time they said that word. Charles couldn't take it anymore. He slammed his body against the scrawniest-looking homeless man, who tumbled to the sidewalk. Charles pushed forward. His foot struck the fallen man's shoulder, but he didn't look back.

"*Narkalooloo hamarammafuckaluck!*" They called out after him. "*Narkalooloo hamarammafuckaluck!*"

He couldn't return to his apartment quickly enough.

* * * *

At the end of the night, he didn't even feel like masturbating.

81

DAY FIVE

AS SOON AS he awoke, Charles reached for the phone on the nightstand to call Tony at the used car lot. He'd intended on asking for time off since it was *Demon Day*. He hadn't signed up for the *festivities*, nor would he be wearing the red tank top that signified participation, but he didn't want to take any chances.

Tony's phone rang and rang. Charles was about to put it down when the other end of the line finally opened.

"Hello."

"Tony?"

"Yeah, this is Tony." Then, with his mouth further from the receiver, he began to sing in a staccato yet sing-songy voice. "T-t-t-tony s-s-s-speakin-n-n-n'."

"Okay, well, this is Charles. I wondered if I could take off work this afternoon. It's *Demon Day* today, so I'd rather not go out unless I absolutely have to."

"Oh sure. Take off, off, off you gooooooooooo!" He held the final 'o' for a good ten seconds.

Charles was surprised that it'd been so easy, and so weird.

"Thanks, Tony. Maybe I'll come in early on **Mon**day."

"No need. No need. Stop by my place later and I'll show you my collection."

The last thing he wanted to see was his boss' collection. "I already told you that I don't feel comfortable going out today."

"Come on over and I'll show you my c-c-c-collection."

"But—"

Tony didn't let him finish before breaking out in extended song. "My c-c-c-collection. Collection. My c-c-c-collection. Collection. Shake that ass, baby! S-s-s-shake it! Yeah!" He began to make drum sounds, wet and sloshy. Charles assumed he was beating his hands against his stomach. "My c-c-c-collection. Collection. *Rock on.*"

He wasn't in the mood to be serenaded by anyone, especially his crazy boss. "That's great and all, but I really have to go. Something's boiling over on the stove."

Tony's voice suddenly lost the sing-songy cadence. "You *will* see my collection."

Charles didn't know how to respond.

"You will see my collection. I'll show it to you." Tony inhaled deeply. "*Today.*"

"But I— I really don't—"

"Such a fine collection it is, Charles. A fine collection indeed. Bountiful. Overflowing. *Fleshy.*"

Charles slammed down the phone and fell back onto the bed. There, he slept for another two hours, dreaming of dark cellars and deep holes and all the slimy things that squirmed down inside them.

* * * *

And he would have slept longer had the phone not rung.

He looked at it with distrust. He feared that it'd be Tony again, demanding in no uncertain terms that he see his collection. Finally, hands near trembling, he lifted the receiver.

"Charles speaking."

He was floored to hear Satan's voice on the other end.

"Satan! Oh my—" He almost said 'god'. "It's been—what?—a month since you last called."

"It has, it has. And I'm sorry for not calling sooner."

"Don't worry about that. I'm just glad to hear your voice."

"And I'm glad to hear yours, too. And guess what, I'm just ten minutes outside of town."

"You mean Chicago?"

"No, I mean Grape City. I'm on the bus as we speak." He paused as though considering his words deeply. "And I should disembark, uh, just in time for *Demon Day*."

Charles exhaled. "So, you've made your decision"

"Don't think less of me, Charles."

He shook his head. For such a one-time powerful be-ing, Satan had very little self-esteem. Charles couldn't imag-ine anything that his ex-boss could do that would make him think less of him. The thought alone was nonsensical. Though he hated that Satan felt compelled to participate, he neverthe-less respected his decision. "Of course I don't think less of you. I'd be glad to have you over."

Satan's voice still sounded wounded. "You didn't write me yesterday."

Now it was Charles' turn to apologize. "Sorry, Satan. I just couldn't think of anything to say. You seemed in such a funk, and I didn't want to make you feel any worse."

"I understand, Charles. Believe me, I do. Even a bad email from you is better than no email, but I guess I'm not one to talk. I haven't written or called much, myself."

"Don't worry about that, either. You've probably had a lot on your mind."

He sighed. "The people in Chicago are totally insane."

"Look on the bright side, Satan. They can't be as bad as they are here."

"I doubt it, Charles. Things are bad. So bad."

Satan's voice sounded more lifeless than ever. A little pick-me-up was in order. "Hey, at the very least we'll be able to see each other again. We don't even have to talk about the bad things. If you want, we could just watch TV."

Charles had to listen closely to hear the rest of Satan's conversation. The other people on the bus were quickly becoming loud and unruly. "I'd like that, Charles," he said. "Very much. You were always my favorite advisor, and I'm glad we still talk."

"Well, thanks. That means a lot coming from you."

"I just wish I could stay longer, but the Chicago bus leaves at 9. I figure we'll have a good hour and a half together after *Demon Day* is over, though."

"An hour and a half is good. And maybe you can come back again in the summer, or I could come and visit you. Maybe I'll have some money saved by then."

"You'd always be welcome here, Charles. My home is your home."

"And vice versa," he added.

"Hey, I brought the last picture I took of Cerebus with me." Satan paused, and Charles heard one of the passengers make baboon noises. "I could show it to you, if you'd like."

He felt a lump in his throat. "Maybe next time, but now is just too soon."

"Okay, Charles. I—"

Charles could no longer hear him. Baboon sounds competed with the din of breaking glass and screeching tires.

"Satan? Satan? Can you hear me?"
Something banged, and all he heard was static.

* * * *

Charles didn't feel like eating, but went to the kitchen anyway. Satan was probably fine, even if the bus had wrecked and killed every human onboard. Still, he hated the thought of the poor guy trapped in an upturned bus with all those flapping loonies, even if they were dead flapping loonies. His condition was too delicate to deal with an event of that magnitude, especially if he'd gotten injured.

From the cabinet, he removed a box of *Shreddy-Puffs*. He opened it and removed a heaping handful. They were okay with milk, but Charles preferred them plain.

He'd popped half the handful in his mouth, and had chewed them for a few seconds, before he realized how vile they tasted—like sewage mixed with semen mixed with lint. He spat them to the floor. The puffs were green and blue as they swam in their spit pool; they were supposed to be yellow. On closer inspection, each puff appeared to have tiny filaments growing from it, filaments that writhed back and forth, up and down. Charles looked into the box and saw that the entire contents had been corrupted.

For the first time in his life, he threw up.

* * * *

Once his stomach settled, Charles brought his chair to the window for another round of people watching.

He opened the window so that he could see and hear

better. There were no cars on the street as that section of road, and a few others he couldn't see, had been cordoned off for *Demon Day*. And there weren't any participants, either. He didn't expect them to show for another ten minutes, but there were a few vendors outside his window, practicing their spiel. One was set up against the building across from him, dressed up like a ringmaster in a glittery red coat and pants and standing beside a large black stone that hadn't been there the night before. His face was made up like that of a circus clown, so Charles couldn't tell if there was anything wrong with it.

"DEMON SEX!" He shouted, reading from a piece of paper. "See freaks extend protuberances from the most unlikely of places! Just ten dollars for DEMON SEX! Get your ass in here or I'll run you through a wood chipper and feed you to the hogs!"

Further down the street, he heard another vendor calling. "Get your MEXOTREXIC-8 here, ladies and gentlemen! Get your MEXOTREXIC-8—pure, uncut, and guaranteed not to cause cerebral hemorrhages or sudden cardiac death!"

He heard a third vendor too, this time so distant that his spiel was nearly inaudible. "FARM PORN! FARM PORN! Red-hot GOATS and succulent SWINE! Supplies are limited!"

Charles was certain that all these booths would be popular.

He looked for, but didn't see, demons hanging from lampposts. That was a good thing, but it didn't mean there weren't any on other streets, their guts filled with candy as stick-wielding children prepared to beat them like living piñatas. Once, he'd seen a child pull off a demon's arm and beat the poor bastard with it rather than use the stick provided. He didn't want to think about how long it'd taken the thing to recover from those wounds.

At least they were paid well for their suffering, and demons tended to be quicker than the humans. Most were able to get out of *Demon Day* with little or no scarring. Still, Charles couldn't imagine himself as a participant. The humiliation alone would be lethal.

The clock on the wall said it was a minute until noon.

He leaned forward, almost so that his head was outside the apartment. He thought he heard stampeding feet in the distance, like the running of the bulls. In a perfect world, it would be the other way around, humans screaming as feet smoldered beneath hot, sulfurous ground. But the world, Charles knew, was very imperfect. Closer and closer, he heard the feet come. It wouldn't be long now.

True to form, the demons arrived on scene first. Charles didn't see Satan in the mix—he hoped his run, provided he wasn't still stuck on the bus, would be on another street—but he did recognize a number of fellow ex-minions, all wearing the usual red tank tops associated with *Demon Day*. He waved at them, as he always did, but they seemed too intent on fleeing to notice. They looked terrified, even though the closest person was probably half a block behind them.

Then the human tide washed by, an amazing lot. Never had he seen so many *Demon Day* participants. It appeared as though the entire city had come out to celebrate. And they didn't stick to the streets. They overran the sidewalks and smashed into the vendors outside, trampling them, crushing their goods, wares, and bones. They hooted and hollered, making noises that sounded neither human nor animal.

And, yes, there was something wrong with their faces— something horrible—but he was too far away to pinpoint exactly what that something was.

At that moment, someone knocked at the door. He'd been so deep in thought that he hadn't heard whoever it was come up the steps.

He froze, and, for a while, didn't even breathe. If he made no sound, he figured whoever it was would think no one was at home and leave. The ploy seemed to work, but then there was another knock.

Let them keep knocking, he thought, and then moved away from the window so the visitor wouldn't spot him on the way out. He just hoped he hadn't been spotted on the way *in*.

A third knock, followed quickly by a voice: "Could you let me in, Terry? I left my lock-picking kit at home. I can be so forgetful sometimes."

It was Helen, the social worker.

Charles wanted to be relieved. She was one of the more non-threatening humans he'd encountered, but so much had changed in the last few days. He wasn't about to allow her or anyone else not named 'Satan' inside. He found himself thinking of vampires and other hideous things that required invitations.

"Please, Henry. I *must* talk with you. I'm dying to know how your date with Jeanine went."

Charles crept quietly across the living room. He didn't want to look out of the peephole; he didn't want to see, but made himself lean over and put his eye to the door.

Helen's face had turned orange, craterous. Patchy hair slithered, snakelike, on her scalp. Everything about her seemed mobile—skin shifting, bubbling, and crawling—like something living had trapped itself inside her skull.

When she spoke again, her lips moved out of sync with

her words. "I know you're in there, Roger. I can smell you."

He backed away from the door.

"Let me in. Don't you want to talk about your date?" Her voice became increasingly high-pitched and shrill. "Your date. Your date. Your date..."

Charles cupped his hands over his ears. "Please, please go away! I'm sick and I can't come to the door!"

"Oh, I'm sick, too. Very, very sick—sick with something *bad*. And I'd love to share it with you."

He fell to the sofa and curled up, like an infant. He closed his eyes and rocked back and forth, trying to wish away both the thing at his door and the crazed and riotous sounds of *Demon Day* outside.

"Don't leave me standing out here. If you do, I'll make note of it in your record, and it won't look good. Oh no, not good at all."

"Make note of it, then!"

"Well, I guess I can't force you to be considerate. Maybe you'll be in a better mood soon."

He listened. Helen's footsteps sounded watery as she descended the stairs. He breathed in and out to calm himself until the door that led out onto the street closed. Then he took the deepest breath of all.

Below, the outside door opened again. The watery footsteps returned.

"Oh, I almost forgot," Helen said as she clumped up the stairs. "I don't need my lock-picker anymore 'cause I can use my body to melt your door." She giggled, but it sounded more like a groan. "Silly me."

Charles looked on as wood began to smoke.

"I'll be right in, Teddy. Just give me a moment."

His eyes darted around the room. There was no other exit save the windows, and no place to hide.

He turned back to the door. It was giving way, slouching on its hinges as though wood were transmuting into molten plastic.

Charles bounded from the sofa, almost tripping multiple times before he reached the bedroom. There, he slammed the door shut and pushed a chest of drawers against it. He feared that it wouldn't work, that Helen would be able to melt right through it, too. At the very least, it'd buy him some time.

Soon, those wet and sloshy footsteps were in the living room.

"I don't know what's gotten you so riled up. You weren't this way last time I visited."

It sounded like she was in the hall now. Charles pressed his back tight against the dresser. It rattled as Helen slammed her fist against the door.

"I just want to talk, Charles. Talk. Talk. Talk. Talk. Talk."

"Please go away! Please leave!"

He felt a sudden burst of heat. The bedroom door was melting along with the chest of drawers.

His back began to burn. He turned and saw his shirt covered in steaming goo. He threw it off, but some of the stuff had burned through to his skin, which was becoming red and inflamed.

There was no time to clean it off. In mere seconds, the chest of drawers had transformed into a noisome, fungoid thing. It tumbled forward and broke open on the floor like a melon. A too-long arm snaked past the door facing. Charles didn't want to see anymore. He bolted to the window, threw it open, and jumped out, landing hard on his knees. He winced, but the pain in his back was far worse.

Looking up, he found himself standing amongst thousands of ex-people. Charles ducked into the *The Machine Shop*. There, mutating customers fused with electronic appliances.

He ducked back out. There was no safe haven; he had to run. All around him, a blur of orange and craterous faces. They surged in every direction, pulling off each other's spongy parts and ramming them into mouths as large as sewer holes. The soles of his shoes began to steam; there was so much goo on the road.

Just ahead of him, another black rock shot up from the pavement. No sooner than it stopped growing did another start. Larger than the last one, it blew out a cloud of dirt and rock in its wake. Dozens more followed suit. No matter where he turned, he found himself faced with a rock or a gibbering, orange horror. He darted past everything, trying not to think of any of it, trying instead to focus on breaking free from the tangled orange and black maze.

The pain in his back became excruciating. He couldn't imagine how the skin there might look. He blocked that out of his mind too, thinking of nothing more than the color gray— bland and comforting. There was no running, eating, jumping, hopping, fucking, or killing in this void. Nothing craterous like the moon or black like obsidian.

Only gray.

* * * *

He had traveled almost twenty blocks before leaving the maze. Streets still brimmed with monstrosities and towering black stones, but not in such numbers that he couldn't run in a straight line. He felt a burn at his feet and tossed off his now molten shoes.

Running barefoot stung, but it didn't compare to the pain in his back. He touched it. The blister there felt as big as a billiard ball, and it stretched and pulled as he moved.

He turned a corner and entered the road that, eventually, would lead him out of town.

He followed it a half-mile before he noticed a glimmer in the distance. At first, he thought it could be anything, a piece of plastic or maybe a sheet of tin. It wasn't until he got closer that he thought it might be the top of a bus.

Closer still, he saw that the thing was mired in a ditch. Charles jumped into that ditch the moment he reached it. There, six feet from the top of the road, he marveled at damage he could now see in full.

The bus must have collided head-on with something large—a Mac Truck, perhaps, or a cement mixer—before finding its way into the ditch, as its nose had been smashed to the middle of the passenger compartment.

Charles climbed in through a broken window. Corpses were strewn about inside. Most injuries appeared crash related. Others didn't, including an instance of genitalia stuffed into a mouth along with a pink party whistle.

He panned his head from side to side, searching each row. The tilt was so extreme that he had to hold onto the edges and sides of seats as he walked. Many of the dead were still human. Others seemed to be in an early stage of transformation. It wasn't until he reached the rear of the bus that he spotted Satan. His old boss was sandwiched between the bathroom wall and the seat in front of him. He appeared more trapped than injured.

For a second, he feared that Satan too had become an orange horror. Then he realized that he'd just let himself go. Heaping fat rows undulated with his breath, buckling cheap thrift store clothing. His hair looked thin, greasy, and unkempt. Further up, one of his horns was missing. Satan, Charles realized, now resembled an obese, slightly reddish human. Even the one horn that remained didn't alter that image.

Charles got down on his hands and knees. "Let's get you off this bus."

"I can't go out."

He leaned in closer. "Are you hurt anywhere?"

Satan nodded.

Charles couldn't tell if his answer had been yes or no. He erred on the side of caution. "Okay, but not so bad that you can't bend these seats back, right?"

Satan said nothing.

"Come on, I know you're still strong enough to do that."

Finally: "I could, but I won't."

It took him a few moments to understand. "Oh no—No—"

"I just want to stay here. Is that too much to ask?"

"Stay until you die, you mean?"

Satan nodded.

"Are you delirious? Did you hit your head?"

"My head's fine."

"Then what's wrong with you!"

"You should know the answer, Charles." He sighed. "I've been as good as dead since the Earth made Hell obsolete."

"If you think that way, then the people win."

"They've already won."

"Just get up." Charles tugged at his shirt. "Get up and we'll find a way out." His mind suddenly flashed back to the night at *The Swinging Lantern*. Had Father Malachi said something important, something about *transformations* and *cities first*? He didn't trust his recollection—the restaurant had been so loud—but, true or not, revealing it could only embolden Satan. "Besides," he said. "I heard something a few days ago, and it makes me think that what happened here hasn't happened everywhere, at least not yet."

"It doesn't matter. Either way, I'm sick of pretending."

Charles tried to force the compressed seat back into place, but wasn't strong enough.

"Please say you don't think less of me."

He wanted to speak, to say *something*. His lips moved, but no sound came out.

"That's all you need to say. Then I can die happy." Satan's head drooped to his shoulders. "Please let me die happy."

Satan, at that moment, seemed just as dead as the other passengers. Charles felt composure crumble as his skin and throat tightened. The ceiling above him appeared, suddenly, to breathe. Panic had leeched in.

He turned and bolted back across the aisle to the window. He squeezed out of it, oblivious to the sting of his popped blister until he was up and out of the ditch.

He ran. Satan called out repeatedly. Charles heard him for longer than he thought possible, but he'd run forever if he had to, past the metropolis and into whatever lie beyond.

* * * *

The outskirts gave way to the suburbs, which soon gave way to the country. He saw trees there—the first he'd seen that weren't on TV or in the park—growing between tired old houses and barren fields.

There weren't many ex-people—the place looked dead—but Charles still ran. He didn't even need to think about running anymore, or about reaching some future destination. He daydreamed his way out of reality as his legs scissored back and forth on pavement.

Charles was dreaming of trees, fast food, and the B-52s when an orange thing shot out onto the street from the side of a church. He never saw it coming. He plowed into the thing, and it exploded in a rainbow of jelly.

Shattered remains quivered at his feet. He didn't see them, either. His eye sockets felt aflame, and he could see nothing but red. His skin and muscles baked. Beneath them, organs seemed to flow like lava.

He staggered into the alley from which the orange thing had emerged. He groped blindly for something to hold onto, but found only air. Breathing first became difficult, then impossible. He fell into a bed of trash, his body twisting and turning, melting away.

DAY SIX

A THIN BEAM of sunlight entered the alley and awoke Charles. For a moment, he thought he was in his apartment and reached over to switch off the alarm before it could beep and become annoying. It wasn't until his hand brushed up against a broken cola bottle that he remembered where he was.

He arose with a jolt, surprised to have a body, much less be alive. His eyes darted around, looking for insane, flapping things, but, apart from him, the alley was empty.

It was also blocked. One of the black stones had shot up between the buildings, sealing off the alley from the street. That meant the things probably wouldn't get to him, but getting out would be difficult, if not impossible.

Charles wasn't sure he even wanted out; that would mean re-entering the world. He sighed and allowed his head to rest against broken and sagging brickwork. He shot up once he noticed that it emitted a yellow, foul smelling gas. The now-spongy bricks didn't burn him, but he didn't want to take chances.

He bent down to wipe dirt and muck from his clothes. They felt slick and leathery beneath his touch, nothing like the undershirt and slacks he expected he'd be wearing. He looked down and saw new clothes—fire-forged chains, straps and buckles, all on a bodysuit so similar to the one he wore in Hell, only this time bright orange instead of black.

And other things were different, too. He ran his hands up and down his sides, confused and uncertain, but it only perplexed him further when certainty finally hit home.

His love handles were smaller.

He felt all over his body. It didn't feature the taunt abs and smooth skin of Hell, but it was a decided improvement over the day before. Even his penis felt somehow wider.

He went over to the rock that blocked his exit, grasped its craggy surface, and began to climb. When he reached the summit, he wasn't nearly as winded as he imagined he'd be.

Looking out, he saw that the rock was but one in a series of peaks that loomed above verdant mountain terrain. The landscape extended beyond his sight, dotted with ruins of man-made structures, but they too were sagging and emitting the yellow gas of decay. He imagined all would disintegrate and that, soon, not even muck would remain.

Charles jumped off the rock and landed on his feet. Confidence increased as he followed a stony path through a crimson, green, and obsidian landscape, marveling at trees that sported wide gaping mouths and flapping tongues. He touched them, and they radiated a true, purposeful blackness into his palm. It was different than Hell's blackness, more focused and driven, but not at all random or insane. That alone relieved him.

Further ahead, Charles came upon a molten stream. A beast like a demonic fawn stood at its banks, lapping up viscous red gel. It turned to him and spoke in an ancient tongue, one he hadn't heard since early demon-hood.

He nodded in understanding at the demon-fawn, and it nodded back. Their connection was short-lived, but the static aftershock lingered for miles.

Charles—though he often thought his old name, *Deraxmuth*—relished the crunch of deep crimson grass beneath his feet. So much thrived in this anti-Garden. It was more *living* than any sphere he'd previously known.

Soon, he reached a clearing where the path ended in a cliff. Charles walked to the precipice and looked down. A vast canyon unfolded beneath him.

Father Malachi was there, sitting atop a column of rock connected by rope-bridge to the mainland and reading a book that, to Charles/*Deraxmuth*'s newly improved eyes, seemed to feature either a clown or a circus midget on its cover. Just doing that, he seemed as awe-inspiring as Satan had in his prime. Sick and pathetic ex-people, however, appeared as ants. They writhed on the canyon floor and there ate of the fruits of their final transformation.

With powers restored, *Deraxmuth*/Charles could look into the fate of Man—provided the thing called *Man* existed on this sphere—but his new boss was *Mystery*. Still, he could *feel* Malachi. While Satan had felt balanced and consistent, Malachi buzzed with the forces of orchestrated chaos and universal change.

He was grateful to him for bringing about the Earth's transformation, but would such an entity need an advisor? Malachi felt so single-minded and purposeful, like a man who refused outside opinion. There were ways to find out, though. The best way, he figured, was to talk to him.

Derax/Char*muth*les went to the other side of the canyon, all the while mulling over the words he might say. He crossed the rope bridge, happy, at least, to live in a world where stupid, frothing animals didn't rut and rape in the streets or graze on fast food and candy without bothering to notice the blood and viscera of the hack-fucked and the rape-slammed.

This, *Muthlerax Chardes* knew, was The Pit.

ABOUT THE AUTHOR

Kevin lives in the hills of Tennessee.

His short fiction and poetry has appeared in such venues as The Mammoth Book of Legal Thrillers, Flesh and Blood, ChiZine, The Cafe Irreal, Poe's Progeny, Book of Dark Wisdom, Dark Discoveries, Bathtub Gin, Not One of Us, Dreams and Nightmares, Electric Velocipede, Sick: An Anthology of Illness, Bust Down the Door and Eat all the Chickens, and others.

He also edits the Bare Bone anthology series for Raw Dog Screaming Press and does not eat chimpanzees.

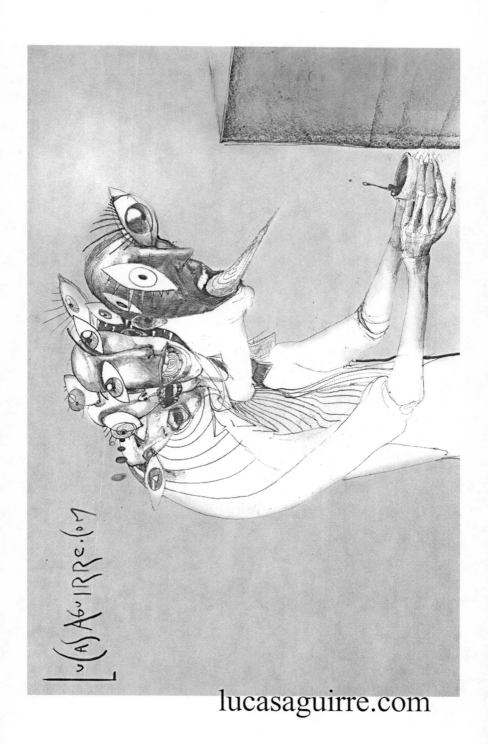

lucasaguirre.com

Bizarro books

CATALOGUE – SPRING 2006

Bizarro Books publishes under the following imprints:

www.rawdogscreamingpress.com

www.eraserheadpress.com

www.afterbirthbooks.com

www.swallowdownpress.com

For all your Bizarro needs visit:

www.bizarrogenre.org

BB-001"The Kafka Effekt" D. Harlan Wilson - A collection of forty-four irreal short stories loosely written in the vein of Franz Kafka, with more than a pinch of William S. Burroughs sprinkled on top.   211 pages $14

BB-002 "Satan Burger"   Carlton Mellick III - The cult novel that put Carlton Mellick III on the map ... Six punks get jobs at a fast food restaurant owned by the devil in a city violently overpopulated by surreal alien cultures.   236 pages $14

BB-003 "Some Things Are Better Left Unplugged" Vincent Sakwoski - Join The Man and his Nemesis, the obese tabby, for a nightmare roller coaster ride into this postmodern fantasy.   152 pages $10

BB-004 "Shall We Gather At the Garden?" Kevin L Donihe - Donihe's Debut novel. Midgets take over the world, The Church of Lionel Richie vs. The Church of the Byrds, plant porn and more!   244 pages $14

BB-005 "Razor Wire Pubic Hair" Carlton Mellick III - A genderless humandildo is purchased by a razor dominatrix and brought into her nightmarish world of bizarre sex and mutilation.   176 pages $11

BB-006 "Stranger on the Loose" D. Harlan Wilson - The fiction of Wilson's 2nd collection is planted in the soil of normalcy, but what grows out of that soil is a dark, witty, otherworldly jungle...   228 pages $14

BB-007 "The Baby Jesus Butt Plug" Carlton Mellick III - Using clones of the Baby Jesus for anal sex will be the hip sex fetish of the future. 92 pages $10

BB-008 "Fishyfleshed" Carlton Mellick III - The world of the past is an illogical flatland lacking in dimension and color, a sick-scape of crispy squid people wandering the desert for no apparent reason. 260 pages $14

BB-009 "Dead Bitch Army" Andre Duza - Step into a world filled with racist teenagers, cannibals, 100 warped Uncle Sams, automobiles with razor-sharp teeth, living graffiti, and a pissed-off zombie bitch out for revenge. 344 pages $16

BB-010 "The Menstruating Mall" Carlton Mellick III *"The Breakfast Club* meets *Chopping Mall* as directed by David Lynch."* - Brian Keene 212 pages $12

BB-011 "Angel Dust Apocalypse" Jeremy Robert Johnson - Meth-heads, manmade monsters, and murderous Neo-Nazis. "Seriously amazing short stories..." - Chuck Palahniuk, author of *Fight Club* 184 pages $11

BB-012 "Ocean of Lard" Kevin L Donihe / Carlton Mellick III - A parody of those old Choose Your Own Adventure kid's books about some very odd pirates sailing on a sea made of animal fat. 176 pages $12

BB-013 "Last Burn in Hell" John Edward Lawson - From his lurid angst-affair with a lesbian music diva to his ascendance as unlikely pop icon the one constant for Kenrick Brimley, official state prison gigolo, is he's got no clue what he's doing. 172 pages $14

BB-014 "Tangerinephant" Kevin Dole 2 - TV-obsessed aliens have abducted Michael Tangerinephant in this bizarro combination of science fiction, satire, and surrealism. 164 pages $11

BB-015 "Foop!" Chris Genoa - Strange happenings are going on at Dactyl, Inc, the world's first and only time travel tourism company.
"A surreal pie in the face!" - Christopher Moore 300 pages $14

BB-016 "Spider Pie" Alyssa Sturgill - A one-way trip down a rabbit hole inhabited by sexual deviants and friendly monsters, fairytale beginnings and hideous endings. 104 pages $11

BB-017 "The Unauthorized Woman" Efrem Emerson - Enter the world of the inner freak, a landscape populated by the pre-dead and morticioners, by cockroaches and 300-lb robots. 104 pages $11

BB-018 "Fugue XXIX" Forrest Aguirre - Tales from the fringe of speculative literary fiction where innovative minds dream up the future's uncharted territories while mining forgotten treasures of the past. 220 pages $16

BB-019 "Pocket Full of Loose Razorblades" John Edward Lawson - A collection of dark bizarro stories. From a giant rectum to a foot-fungus factory to a girl with a biforked tongue. 190 pages $13

BB-020 "Punk Land" Carlton Mellick III - In the punk version of Heaven, the anarchist utopia is threatened by corporate fascism and only Goblin, Mortician's sperm, and a blue-mohawked female assassin named Shark Girl can stop them. 284 pages $15

BB-021 "Pseudo-City" D. Harlan Wilson - Pseudo-City exposes what waits in the bathroom stall, under the manhole cover and in the corporate boardroom, all in a way that can only be described as mind-bogglingly irreal. 220 pages $16

BB-022 "Kafka's Uncle and Other Strange Tales" Bruce Taylor - Anslenot and his giant tarantula (tormentor? fri-end?) wander a desecrated world in this novel and collection of stories from Mr. Magic Realism Himself. 348 pages $17

BB-023 "Sex and Death In Television Town" Carlton Mellick III - In the old west, a gang of hermaphrodite gunslingers take refuge from a demon plague in Telos: a town where its citizens have televisions instead of heads. 184 pages $12

BB-024 "It Came From Below The Belt" Bradley Sands - What can Grover Goldstein do when his severed, sentient penis forces him to return to high school and help it win the presidential election? 204 pages $13

BB-025 "Sick: An Anthology of Illness" John Lawson, editor - These Sick stories are horrendous and hilarious dissections of creative minds on the scalpel's edge. 296 pages $16

BB-026 "Tempting Disaster" John Lawson, editor - A shocking and alluring anthology from the fringe that examines our culture's obsession with taboos. 260 pages $16

BB-027 "Siren Promised" Jeremy Robert Johnson - Nominated for the Bram Stoker Award. A potent mix of bad drugs, bad dreams, brutal bad guys, and surreal/incredible art by Alan M. Clark. 190 pages $13

BB-028 "Chemical Gardens" Gina Ranalli - Ro and punk band *Green is the Enemy* find Kreepkins, a surfer-dude warlock, a vengeful demon, and a Metal Priestess in their way as they try to escape an underground nightmare. 188 pages $13

 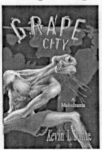  

BB-029 "Jesus Freaks" Andre Duza For God so loved the world that he gave his only two begotten sons... and a few million zombies. 400 pages $16

BB-030 "Grape City" Kevin L. Donihe - More Donihe-style comedic bizarro about a demon named Charles who is forced to work a minimum wage job on Earth after Hell goes out of business. 108 pages $10

BB-031"Sea of the Patchwork Cats" Carlton Mellick III - A quiet dreamlike tale set in the ashes of the human race. For Mellick enthusiasts who also adore *The Twilight Zone*. 112 pages $10

BB-032 "Extinction Journals" Jeremy Robert Johnson 104 pages - An uncanny voyage across a newly nuclear America where one man must confront the problems associated with loneliness, insane dieties, radiation, love, and an ever-evolving cockroach suit with a mind of its own. 104 pages $10

BB-033 "Meat Puppet Cabaret" Steve Beard At last! The secret connection between Jack the Ripper and Princess Diana's death revealed! **240 pages** **$16 / $30**

BB-034 "The Greatest Fucking Moment in Sports" Kevin L. Donihe - In the tradition of the surreal anti-sitcom *Get A Life* comes a tale of triumph and agape love from the master of comedic bizarro. **108 pages** **$10**

BB-035 "The Troublesome Amputee" John Edward Lawson - Disturbing verse from a man who truly believes nothing is sacred and intends to prove it. **104 pages** **$9**

BB-036 "Deity" Vic Mudd God (who doesn't like to be called "God") comes down to a typical, suburban, Ohio family for a little vacation—but it doesn't turn out to be as relaxing as He had hoped it would be... **168 pages** **$12**

BB-037 "The Haunted Vagina" Carlton Mellick III - It's difficult to love a woman whose vagina is a gateway to the world of the dead. **132 pages** **$10**

BB-038 "Tales from the Vinegar Wasteland" Ray Fracalossy - Witness: a man is slowly losing his face, a neighbor who periodically screams out for no apparent reason, and a house with a room that doesn't actually exist. **240 pages** **$14**

BB-039 "Suicide Girls in the Afterlife" Gina Ranalli - After Pogue commits suicide, she unexpectedly finds herself an unwilling "guest" at a hotel in the Afterlife, where she meets a group of bizarre characters, including a goth Satan, a hippie Jesus, and an alien-human hybrid. **100 pages** **$9**

BB-040 "And Your Point Is?" Steve Aylett - In this follow-up to LINT multiple authors provide critical commentary and essays about Jeff Lint's mind-bending literature. **104 pages** **$11**

BB-041 "Not Quite One of the Boys" Vincent Sakowski -While drug-dealer Maxi drinks with Dante in purgatory, God and Satan play a little tri-level chess and do a little bargaining over his business partner, Vinnie, who is still left on earth. **220 pages** **$14**

COMING SOON:

"Misadventures in a Thumbnail Universe" by Vincent Sakowski

"House of Houses" by Kevin Donihe

"War Slut" by Carlton Mellick III

ORDER FORM

TITLES	QTY	PRICE	TOTAL
Shipping costs (see below)			
TOTAL			

Please make checks and moneyorders payable to ROSE O'KEEFE / BIZARRO BOOKS in U.S. funds only. Please don't send bad checks! Allow 2-6 weeks for delivery. International orders may take longer. If you'd like to pay online via PAYPAL.COM, send payments to publisher@eraserheadpress.com.

SHIPPING: US ORDERS - $2 for the first book, $1 for each additional book. For priority shipping, add an additional $4. INT'L ORDERS - $5 for the first book, $3 for each additional book. Add an additional $5 per book for global priority shipping.

Send payment to:

BIZARRO BOOKS
C/O Rose O'Keefe
205 NE Bryant
Portland, OR 97211

Name

Address

City   State   Zip

Country

Email   Phone

Printed in the United States
129176LV00001B/202/P